Searching For Love

Pride, Oregon
Book 16

Jill Sanders

DIGITAL ISBN: 978-1-945100-95-6

PRINT ISBN: 979-8-884971-39-4

Text copyright © 2024 Grayton Press

Copyeditor: Erica Ellis–inkdeepediting.com

Summary

Can Avery fix her own heart and find the love she's been missing?

Head back to Pride, Oregon, to find out what some of your favorite Jill Sanders' characters are up to.

Avery has always been the go-to person in her hometown, the one who can fix anything and everything. But when Lucas comes to town, she realizes that something is missing in her life. Lucas is everything she's ever wanted in a man: charming, passionate, and adventurous. As they spend more time together, Avery begins to wonder if she's been missing true love all along.

Lucas has left his old life behind to start anew, and Avery is just the woman to make it all worthwhile. But as they navigate their budding romance, he'll have to confront the demons of his past. Will Avery be able to let go of her need to fix everything and let Lucas into her heart? Can

Lucas convince her that he's worth taking a chance on? Find out in this heartwarming romance about two people who discover that love is the ultimate fixer-upper.

Prologue

Avery Ann Auston was thirteen when she discovered her hidden talent. Her purpose in life. No, she couldn't sing, nor could she make amazing art that would make her famous. Her talent was to fix things and help people.

Whenever someone around her had a problem, Avery stepped in and the problem went away. This was not only beneficial to the person she was helping, it was also instrumental to her. She didn't know if it was the endorphins that she got from making others happy or if it was just the feeling of being needed.

Whatever the reason, from that moment on, she set her sights on being Pride, Oregon's go-to girl.

By the age of eighteen, she had gone through more jobs than she could remember. She was pretty sure that she had worked at every single business in the small town by the time she'd graduated high school.

It wasn't until that fateful day during one of Pride's Christmas tree lighting celebrations that she realized just what her life was missing.

Chapter One

Holding her breath, Avery felt her best friend Hannah Crawford, soon to be Hannah Auston, beside her and pushed her body even faster. There was no way she was going to lose this time. Not again.

Sure, Hannah had a few inches on her, and gosh, her legs seemed to be far longer than her own. But they had both taken swimming classes, and she knew full well that she could beat her to the shoreline.

Breathless, the pair of them surfaced at the same time and raced to the edge of the water. An avid runner, Avery far outshined Hannah on land. Three days a week, Avery woke at dawn and jogged around the small town that had always been her home.

Sure, the town was only three miles wide, but she weaved through the streets to hit her five-mile mark.

When her feet touched dry sand first, she shouted with joy and started jumping up and down, her arms up in the air as she boasted her greatness loudly to the world.

Her long wet red hair flowed around her shoulders as she leapt about in her victory dance.

Then her brother rushed across the sand towards her, holding up a towel as he yelled her name.

"Jesus, Ave!" Wyatt shoved the towel over her shoulders. "You lost your swimsuit top somewhere!" he growled as he held onto her to stop her from bouncing about.

Avery glanced down at herself and, sure enough, her swimsuit top was nowhere to be found. Her shouts of joy turned to giggles, which turned to hysterical laughter.

Scanning the beach, she realized that there were more than two dozen beachgoers within view. Then she spotted a pair of dark eyes watching her from across the sand and froze. Everything except those eyes faded away in her mind.

How many nights since last Christmas had she dreamed of seeing them again?

Lucas.

Lucas Jenkins.

His smile was contagious. His eyes heated as he looked at her from across the beach. His dark hair was wet as if he'd been in the water moments before.

He was wearing a pair of black swim trunks with a blue stripe down the sides of it and nothing else. A god. He was a god.

Tanned. Toned. Muscular. Dangerous.

Then everything caught up with her and she realized that she'd just flashed everyone on the beach. Including Lucas.

A half gasp, half scream escaped her lips, and she turned away and allowed her brother to cover her completely.

"How in the hell did you lose your top?" Wyatt growled in her ear.

"You lost your top?" Hannah asked a little breathless. "How did you lose your top? I tied it myself."

Hannah's one-piece suit was still intact. The swimsuit Avery had worn to the beach that day was older. It still fit but the elastic was a little loose. She had plans to replace it, really she did.

She'd taken several trips to the mall in search of another "perfect" bikini. But everything made her look either too big or too small up top. Several even pushed her completely flat.

It wasn't that she had really big boobs, but what she did have, she wanted to show off with her chosen swimwear. If she had it, she was going to highlight it.

"Here it is," a deep voice said next to her.

Before she turned, she knew exactly who had found her swimsuit top.

Lucas.

It had been almost six months since she'd last seen him. He'd been working at one of the food trucks for the annual Pride Christmas tree lighting.

They'd flirted. Talked. Exchanged social media contacts. He'd told her he was working at a restaurant in the mall in Edgeview, so she had gone there almost every weekend, hoping to bump into him there. But he hadn't been working when she'd dropped by.

Nor had he updated his location or status on social media.

She knew most guys didn't get into that sort of thing, and apparently, that was true for him too.

"Thanks," her brother said, shoving it at her and then holding up the towel for her so she could put the top back on. "No more going in the water," Wyatt said firmly once she was done, then he smiled, took Hannah's hand, and strolled back towards their towels.

Hannah smiled at her and gave her a little thumbs-up when Lucas remained near her.

"I'm sorry about the show," Avery blurted out.

Lucas's smile was quick.

"You could have charged every guy on the beach for it." He nodded. "I think some of the moms were upset though." He motioned to a group of women who were staring at her with daggers in their eyes as their husbands all tried to avoid looking in her direction. Heat flooded her face and made her wish she could just disappear. "I've been hoping to run into you again," Lucas added.

"You have?" She suddenly felt breathless as she continued to hold the towel her brother had given her around her shoulders.

Lucas nodded. "Care for a walk?" He motioned with his head towards the beach.

"Sure," she said and fell in step with him. After a few steps, she felt stupid about hiding the top half of her body when he'd just seen, well, everything, and she tossed the towel towards her things as they passed them.

"Are you still working at the coffee shop?" Lucas asked, glancing at her sideways.

"Yes." She smiled. "And the pizza shop and the restaurant and—" His chuckle stopped her. "What about you? Are you still working at the restaurant in the mall?"

He shook his head. "Nope, just put a down payment on a building to open my very own restaurant."

"What?" She stopped walking and turned towards him. "Seriously?"

He chuckled and then dipped his chin in a slight nod. The sound of his chuckle did things to her insides. Things that had her face heating.

"Where? In Edgeview?"

"Nope, right here in Pride." He beamed.

"Seriously?" She felt like she was repeating herself. "What kind of restaurant?"

"Well, since I'm a quarter Mexican, I figured... Italian," he said with a chuckle.

She laughed with him at his joke and felt her stomach growl at the thought of food. Pride had never had a Mexican restaurant before. The thought of having a new option excited her, and she knew it would be the same with many others in town. "Are you any good at running your own business?"

He stopped and motioned for them to sit in the sand. After they got comfortable, he answered.

"I have been working nonstop for the past two years at Eddie's. I'm the one who suggested he get a food truck and start sending us out to local events to spread the word. I've been doing books, hiring, firing, orders, you name it." He shrugged. "Everything but taking home the fat paycheck."

She was smiling as he talked. There was no doubt in her mind that he loved his work. No doubt that he was good at it either. She had, after all, sampled the food he'd made during the Christmas festival.

"What building did you purchase?" she asked, feeling stupid that she hadn't asked before.

His smile grew. "The old two-story across from the gas station."

She frowned. "The one next to Sassy and Classy?"

He nodded. "That's the one."

"But I thought they were going to tear it down. Isn't it condemned?"

"Not condemned, just... in need of some TLC." His smile never wavered.

"And you can do that? All the repairs yourself?" She

dug her toes into the sand when she realized that she'd let Georgia Stevens, one of the many kids in town that she babysat, paint her toenails the night before. Currently, each one of her toenails was a different color.

She should have noticed earlier. She should have repainted them when she'd gotten home.

"God, no, not everything. I can do the basics. Hammer, paint." He shrugged. "For the plumbing and electric, I've hired Parker Clark and his crew. They're looking the building over from foundation to roof and starting work later this week."

Avery nodded. She knew Parker well. She babysat the man's kids—twins Ethan and Ellie and their baby brother, Liam—often enough. He had the best handyperson business in town. "Wise choice. Well, if you need any help..." She let her offer drop.

What was she doing? Her schedule was full as it was. She worked as a dispatcher at the fire station one day a week, the Boys and Girls Club two days a week, not to mention filling in at Baked, Sara's Nook, The Brew-Ha-Ha, and the Golden Oar restaurant, and even sometimes down at city hall. Then there were all her friends that she babysat for whenever they called.

When did she have time to help a hunky guy, her dream guy, paint and work on his new building?

Then he smiled at her, and she knew that she would make the time.

"Thanks, I might take you up on that offer. If only I had your phone number?" He sighed for show. "We exchanged social media info, but I neglected to get your actual digits."

"If you have your phone, I can put my contact info in it," she offered.

He shook his head. "My phone is back there with my

things." Then his smile grew and she felt her heart skip a beat. "Tell me your number."

Her eyebrows shot up in question. "Okay." She leaned on her knees and rattled off the seven digits.

He narrowed his eyes and then to her surprise, with a voice that sent waves of goose bumps over her skin, sang her number back to her in a rhythm that she doubted she would ever get out of her head.

"How did you do that?" she asked in awe.

He leaned back on his elbows and shrugged. "My grandfather was in a famous mariachi band."

"Oh?" She leaned back next to him as he talked about how his grandfather traveled the world, playing the guitar with his four best friends until they were in their late sixties.

"The only reason they stopped was because two of the band members died. It sort of broke my grandfather. He stopped playing and stuck closer to home after that." He shrugged and then sighed as he leaned forward. "I'm named after him. Lucas Manuel." He smiled. "I also got his nose." He touched his nose.

"I got my mother's nose and hair." She touched her now dry red hair, which no doubt was in tangles thanks to her swim. She should have braided it earlier.

"What about your blue eyes?" He leaned a little closer, and she felt her heart race as she met his dark chocolate brown eyes.

"Yes, those too." She leaned a little closer until they were a breath away from one another.

"The freckles?" he asked. She nodded. His eyes moved down to her lips, and she held her breath.

Just then a spray of sand flew over the pair of them as her brother came crashing onto the beach inches from their feet, a football in his hands. He laughed while he kept one eye locked on Lucas.

Avery knew the look Wyatt was giving the man. A "keep your lips off my sister" kind of look.

Avery's eyes narrowed as she shot him warning looks.

"Do you play?" Wyatt asked Lucas as he dusted the sand off himself.

Lucas shot her a look.

"My brother." She threw her hands up. "Wyatt."

Lucas nodded. "We've met. I'll play if Avery does." He stood up suddenly and held out his hand for her.

"Avery," Wyatt groaned and tossed the ball to Lucas. Then her brother perked up and added quickly. "Fine, but she's on our team."

Chapter Two

How could someone so small be so good at football? Not only could she easily outthrow him, but she was also easily twice as fast as anyone else playing.

Avery was quite literally running circles around him and her brother. Whenever she scored, she did this sexy little booty dance that had his heart rate spiking and his mind going foggy.

The higher the score went, the more Wyatt laughed at him.

"You play dirty," Lucas told the man after he'd tossed the ball to Avery, who scored the winning points.

"It pays to know who you're up against." Wyatt slapped him on the shoulder.

"Next time we play, I get your sister," he joked, and Wyatt laughed. "Blood is thicker than..."—Wyatt's eyes narrowed slightly—"hormones."

Lucas laughed. "Avery mentioned you got engaged a few months ago."

Wyatt nodded as his eyes moved over to Hannah, his

fiancée. Everything about the man changed. His smile grew when Hannah glanced in their direction across the sand.

"I never thought I'd get so lucky," Wyatt said under his breath. "Which reminds me." He turned to Lucas. "Here's the standard brother talk. Hurt my sister and I'll pound you into the ground."

The fact that Wyatt said this with a smile had him laughing. "I have a younger sister too. I get it."

Wyatt's eyebrows shot up. "How much younger?"

"Ten years." Lucas smiled. "Sophia just turned sixteen." He shifted as Avery and Hannah started walking towards them.

"They're best friends," Wyatt warned. "If Hannah doesn't like you, that door shuts for good."

Avery and Hannah were like night and day. Avery's pale perfect skin and bright red hair reminded him of a painting of a mermaid he'd once seen. Hannah was more, well, standard-looking, he supposed. She had sandy blonde hair and tanned skin. About the only thing that the friends had in common was their blue eyes and the fact that they both wore blue bikinis.

"So, you went MIA for months and suddenly showed up just in time for summer fun?" Hannah said to him as she stopped beside Wyatt and wrapped her arms around the man's waist.

"MIA?" he asked. "Not sure about that." He smiled. "I worked double shifts almost every day for the past few months so I could buy the building down the street from your fiancé's store." He motioned towards Wyatt.

Hannah's eyes narrowed. "Which building?"

"Lucas just bought the old sandwich shop building," Avery said cheerfully.

"I thought they were going to tear that building down?" Wyatt asked.

"Nope, she's solid enough. According to the inspection I paid for, anyway," Lucas said.

"What are you going to do with it?" Wyatt asked.

"Open my own restaurant," he answered quickly.

"What kind?" Hannah asked.

"Authentic Mexican," Avery answered for him.

"Oh my god. That sounds incredible. I could go for some empanadas right about now," Hannah said, holding her stomach.

"Well, as a fellow business owner, let me know if you need anything." Wyatt wrapped his arm around Hannah.

"Will you cater?" Hannah asked.

"I... can," he answered after quickly thinking about it. He'd quit his job in Edgeview and had moved into the small one-room apartment above where the restaurant would go to save money while he renovated. "What's the occasion?"

"Our wedding." Hannah motioned between her and Wyatt. "Next month. We were going to have the Golden Oar handle it but haven't agreed on anything yet. I'd love to do something different." Hannah nudged Wyatt. "Wouldn't it be great to do something unique?"

"Yeah." Wyatt nodded. "We can talk details later. If you think you can handle cooking for two hundred guests just over a month from now?"

"Sure, no problem." He frowned. "However, I'm not sure I'll have a working kitchen at my place yet."

"That's no problem," Hannah said. She looked around and shouted, "Kara!" She waved towards a brunette woman sitting across the sand with a group of others, including a couple of kids. The woman stood up and started towards them. "Kara, this is Lucas. Lucas, Kara."

The pair of them laughed.

"What?" Hannah frowned.

"We're..." Lucas started.

"Cousins," Kara finished.

"You are?" Hannah blushed.

"Lucas Jenkins," he said easily. "Kara and Robin are one of the main reasons I picked Pride to open my new restaurant." He threw an arm over his cousin as he motioned towards the rest of the family, who he'd been hanging out with when Avery and Hannah had emerged from the water.

Robin was seven months pregnant and had yet to stand up from her spot under the umbrella. She appeared as if she was fast asleep at the moment. He was only at the beach that day because they'd invited him along.

"Of course you are." Hannah took an elbow in the ribs from Avery.

"I told you this like a dozen times," Avery hissed.

"Right." Hannah rolled her eyes. "Well, we're having our wedding at your cousins' venue in a little over a month. There's a large kitchen. We're thinking of having Lucas cater the wedding," she told Kara.

"Oh, how wonderful." Kara gasped. "Of course, you can use our kitchens. Just let us know what you need."

He nodded. Was this happening?

Had he just secured a big job before he even had a chance to open his restaurant doors?

"I'd like that," he said eagerly. He hadn't expected to work before the restaurant was open. Then again, the extra money would be worth it. And if he pulled the wedding off, the entire town of Pride would get a taste of what he had to offer.

Just then, Robin crossed the sand towards them, holding Kara's daughter, Reagan, in her arms. His cousin's round belly stuck out in front of her, and she looked very uncomfortable, even after Kara took her daughter from her sister's arms.

Immediately, Reagan's chubby hands reached for him and he easily took her into his arms and put her on his hip.

"Lucas has just secured the catering gig for their wedding," Kara told Robin.

"That's wonderful." Robin smiled as she laid a hand over her belly. "He is by far the best cook in the family."

Kara laughed. "He got that from his dad's side of the family."

"We can't wait," Hannah said.

"Maybe you should prepare some samples?" Avery added as she ran a fingertip down Reagan's chubby cheek. "You know, to narrow down what you want?" she said to Hannah.

"That's a great idea," Kara chimed in. "How about... dinner." She narrowed her eyes at him. "We don't have an event on Saturday after three o'clock. We can meet with you to go over a few more details and then you can enjoy dinner after."

"This weekend?" he asked, and she nodded quickly.

"Are you both available?" Kara asked Hannah and Wyatt. They both quickly nodded.

"You should come too. As my maid of honor, your say in the food is important." Hannah took Avery's hand in hers.

"I wouldn't miss it," Avery said, her eyes locked with his.

It was obvious why he was drawn to her. The kindness was clear in her eyes. Beyond her outer beauty, Avery was pure goodness to her core.

He'd always been drawn to it. Maybe it was his crappy childhood that had opened his eyes to the manipulators of the world. He could tell when people were using him or wanted to gain something from his friendship.

Here, in this group, there weren't any hidden agendas.

While the group of friends continued to chat about the wedding plans, he tried to think of a menu of choices that he could make for them.

He doubted tacos would be the best solution for a fancy event. Still, there were enough authentic items in his grandpa's arsenal of recipes that he'd learned as a kid to impress them.

By the time Wyatt, Hannah, and Avery left, his brain hurt from considering the possibilities.

"Help," he said to Kara and Robin. "Why did I agree to cater a wedding a month away when I haven't even opened my restaurant yet?" He felt a little breathless.

His cousin chuckled as he sat down in the sand with Reagan fast asleep on his chest.

Robin and Kara were his cousins on his mother's side. His mother and Robin and Kara's father were siblings.

Growing up, he'd always felt like his family were the oddballs in the Jenkins family. His parents had never married and shortly after Sophia's sixth birthday, his father had disappeared from their lives.

His grandpa was the only steady male role model in his life, and he had molded him into what he was today. An excellent chef. Someone who stood up for those weaker than he was.

When he'd reached out to his cousins after they'd moved to Pride, he was happily surprised by how welcoming they had been. Not only to him but to his mother and sister.

Lucas's mother worked two jobs in Edgeview. She still

lived in the small three-bedroom home by the hospital that he'd grown up in.

When he'd been old enough, he'd taken odd jobs to help pay the bills. Then, after turning eighteen, he'd needed space and had moved into a small studio apartment, but he'd still helped his mother make ends meet. Even now, he planned to help her out after he opened the restaurant.

He'd seen firsthand the destruction his father's abuse had caused not only to himself but to his mother. Sophia had been too young when their father left for the last time to remember much.

"Lucas, you can do this with your eyes closed. Make what you did for us the last time we visited your mother," Kara said, touching his arm. "Now, give me my sleepy child. I think it's time we went home." She motioned to her husband, Conner, who walked over and gently took Reagan from his arms.

He instantly missed the warmth and softness of the sleeping baby against his chest. He missed the days when he'd watched Sophia when she was younger. Being a big brother was the best feeling in the world. It had trained him for the day when he'd have a half dozen kids himself.

He daydreamed about those six kids the entire drive back into town, and the fact that they all had fiery red hair and crystal blue eyes did little to calm his fears about cooking for Avery and her best friend and brother.

This was probably the most important thing he'd do in his entire life. He just had to get this one right. His future, and that of those six red-headed kids, depended on it.

Chapter Three

Avery knew that it would look like she was desperate to see Lucas again if she stopped by his building the following day. But after working a half shift at the bakery, she figured she'd just... walk by. And after her and Lucas's eyes met through the large glass window, well, it would be rude of her not to say hi. Right?

If the smile on Lucas's lips was any indication, he was pleased to see her as well.

She stopped on the sidewalk and waited as he unlocked the old wood and glass doors. An ancient bell chimed when he held it open for her.

"Hey," he said a little breathlessly. He was wearing worn jeans and a gray T-shirt that was covered in a layer of dust. There was a smudge of dirt on his chin which made him look even sexier. Most importantly, he looked completely happy.

"Hey," she replied, looking around the dirty room. She could see the potential even through the layers of dirt and trash. "Wow." She stepped in and turned a circle.

"I just moved in two days ago," he pointed out. "First is

cleaning and clearing so Parker and his crew can get in here. Hopefully, they can start the important things tomorrow." He motioned to the full trash bags that lined the back hallway.

"Need any help?" she offered. "I have the rest of the day off and tomorrow as well."

She'd wanted to offer to help him clean up the building when she'd run into him the day before at the beach, but she'd been afraid that she'd sound too eager.

"I'd love some help," Lucas said easily. Then he frowned down at her outfit. "You should probably change first."

She tapped her backpack with a grin. "I have a change of clothes in here. I can change in the bathroom." She motioned to the hallway, remembering where the bathrooms were from when she used to eat there when the place was Bonnie's Sandwich Shop. Actually, for a summer, she had worked behind the counter making sandwiches as well.

"Great," Lucas said. A pile of trash bags started falling over when she stepped past them. "I'm going to haul these out to the dumpster in the alley," he suggested while she disappeared into the bathroom to change into the clothes she'd packed in hopes of this exact moment happening.

After pulling on a pair of worn jeans and an oversized T-shirt from the fire station where her dad was the fire chief, she stepped out just in time to help Lucas pull the rest of the trash bags to the dumpster.

"There, now we can move around a little better in here." He dusted off his hands.

"Where do you want to start?" She looked around.

There was still a lot of trash lying around from the dozen years that the place had sat empty.

"Hauling out the trash is my main focus for now." He

picked up a roll of large black trash bags. "While I take care of that, you could sweep?" he suggested.

"Perfect." She walked over and took one of the three brooms he had leaning against the wall. "So," she said after they had started working, "how much in here are you going to change?"

He glanced up from scooping a pile of newspapers into a trash bag and was silent for a moment. "A lot." He sighed as he looked around the room. "Fresh paint everywhere. New booths, tables, chairs." He motioned with his elbow. "Floors will need work." His eyes landed on hers. "That's just out here. The kitchen..." He rolled his eyes. "And upstairs..." He smiled. "That's why I hired Parker."

"Well, I can clean, and paint, and I helped my parents sand and stain their hardwood flooring once." She beamed proudly. "I'll bet this floor just needs some TLC as well."

"I planned on it. I don't have the money yet to replace it." He frowned down at the hardwood.

"We'll get it gleaming like new." She started sweeping again.

For the next hour, while they completely cleared out and cleaned the main dining area's floors, they chatted about his plans for the space. She liked his plan to have brightly colored booths with decorative blown-glass lights over each.

He told her about his friend who was a glassmaker and then showed her a few of the women's pieces while they sat down on the curb and enjoyed a cool drink.

She tried not to be jealous of the way he talked about the other woman. That was until she saw an image of the woman he was talking about. She was in her sixties.

"She's a friend of my grandpa," he added. "I think that there was more between them at one point." He smiled.

"They both deny it, but..." He tucked his phone into his back pocket.

"Does he live in Edgeview?" she asked, curious.

"Between here and Edgeview. He sticks close to my mom and Sophia."

"He's your dad's father?"

He nodded again. "His family is long gone. He's always thought of my mother as his daughter. I think he would have rather..." he started but dropped off with a shake of his head.

"I take it things were difficult?" She laid a hand over his hand.

He smiled. "Things were better when my dad wasn't around. Still, I'm thankful my grandpa was there. He's great with Sophia as well. She takes violin lessons from him."

"He plays?" she asked.

"My grandpa plays all instruments of the heart," he said in a thick accent, most likely mimicking the man himself.

She chuckled. "I'd like to meet him."

"You will, tomorrow. He and my mom will be here to help around the place." He glanced around. "If you're still set for helping tomorrow?"

"I have nothing else to do." She hid a smile.

"We can start in the kitchen," he suggested as he lifted his face to the sun.

"What are you going to do with this area?" she asked, motioning to the small alley they were sitting in.

"This?" He frowned. "Right, I own this entire alley."

"You could always add some string lights and put a few tables out here," she suggested. "Switch that side door out for a glass one so waiters can come and go? There's even room for a stage for a band or karaoke."

"That's a great idea." He jumped up and walked around

the area as if seeing it with renewed vision. "There might be room for a band here." He motioned. "Live music." He snapped his fingers. "Something no one else in town has."

Her heart swelled at the thought. He was right. No other restaurant in town had live music.

Suddenly, he pulled her up from her spot on the curb and spun her around.

"There's even enough room here to dance." He laughed as she laughed with him.

They were breathless when the Myers, an older couple that she'd known her entire life, strolled by with their schnauzer, Buster, and saw them.

"Afternoon," Lucas said joyfully. "Nice day for dancing."

Mrs. Myer smiled while Mr. Myer frowned profusely. Then again, the man always frowned.

"I don't think they were impressed," Lucas whispered when the couple continued walking.

"Don't worry, Mr. Myer is never impressed with anything I do. I suppose that's why he gave me a C in geography class," she joked.

Lucas sighed. "It must be nice knowing everyone in town." He held the door open for her as they stepped back into the building.

"Yes and no. It has its downsides," she admitted. "For one, I could never get away with anything. The one time I thought I had, I strolled into the house to find out that my parents had been called by three do-gooders"—she air quoted—"to inform them of my misdeeds."

"What had you done?" he asked, leaning a little closer to her.

"I don't know you well enough to tell you. Yet," she teased.

"Fair enough." He nodded quickly. "I once tore the head off my rival's mascot and replaced it with a really big stuffed bear head." He smiled. "Never got caught though. I guess there weren't any do-gooders"—he mimicked her air-quoting move—"who cared to call my mother."

She threw up her hands. "I stole Cilla."

"Cilla?"

She took a deep breath. "Cilla was a pig that our sixth-grade class had raised for our 4H project. After I found out that she was going to be slaughtered if she didn't win the blue ribbon, I stole her, took her on a very long walk, and then released her into the Miller's field."

"What happened?" he asked, leaning on the counter that she was currently wiping down without realizing she was doing so.

"Mr. Miller returned Cilla to the 4H barn and, when Cilla won second place, he purchased her himself and she lived happily ever after on the Miller farm until she died of old age." She smiled happily.

"So, something good came of your misdeeds. Trust me, nothing good ever came of me replacing a mascot's ram head with that from a life-sized stuffed bear." He chuckled.

They'd grown up so close to each other, but talking with him for the next hour, she realized how different their child-hoods had been.

While she had been sheltered and raised by a village of townspeople here in Pride, Lucas had struggled with a broken family. According to him, he'd had a difficult time staying out of trouble while he raised himself. Later, he spent most of his time helping to raise his sister while his mother worked several jobs.

After she and Wyatt were born, Avery's mother hadn't worked a job for years. Then, when Avery got her first job, her mother had started managing the accounting for the fire department. Her father said it was to help him out so he didn't have to do it, but they all knew that her mother was going stir-crazy without much to do now that she and her brother were grown.

Shortly after that, several other businesses in town signed her mother on to do their books, and currently, her mother was the accountant for a dozen small businesses in Pride.

"Who is going to do your books?" she asked, leaning on the counter. "My mother is an accountant."

Lucas shifted slightly. "Then she's hired. I haven't thought much beyond fixing all of this up first. I can handle the basics, I have in past jobs, but owning a place, it's different."

She leaned back. "You do have a name picked out for the business, right?"

He shrugged. "Lucas's?" It came out more as a question than an answer.

"Are you asking me?" she asked with a chuckle. He nodded slightly. "Okay, you need a name." She glanced around the room, narrowing her eyes slightly as she imagined his vision. Bright colored booths, colorful glass lights overhead, gleaming hardwood floors, and bright pictures on the walls.

Once everything was done, it would be so colorful. So cheerful. So bright.

"Whatever you decide, it should be as cheerful as you plan on making it in here," she said, a million ideas flooding her mind. Then she snapped her fingers. "What was your grandfather's band's name?"

He tilted his head and then laughed. "Bandidas de Amor. The love bandits."

She laughed. "I bet they broke a lot of hearts."

He nodded. "The living members still do."

"Well, it's a great name for a band of male singers, but not a restaurant." She started pacing behind the counter. "I suppose the name will come to you. We can start a list." She walked over to the old chalkboard that still hung behind the countertop and wrote down a few of her favorite ideas. She added a couple that Lucas suggested. "We can have your family and friends vote on their favorite," she suggested.

"Sounds great," he said quietly.

"Unless you have something you like the most?" she asked. She put a tick mark by her favorite, then set the chalk down. Buen Provecho, which translated to "enjoy your meal."

He walked over and put another check by her choice. "It's something my grandpa always says before a meal." He smiled. "Do you speak Spanish?"

"Sí, un poco." She held up her fingers pinched together, indicating a little bit.

He smiled. "Thanks to my grandpa, I know enough to be dangerous." His smile turned her knees weak.

How was she supposed to concentrate around his family the next day if he kept smiling at her like that?

"I think we're done for the evening. We've lost the light and there's no power down here yet," he said, dusting off his hands. "How about we head over to Baked and I'll buy you a pizza for your efforts?"

"Sounds good. I'll just go freshen up first." She motioned towards the bathroom.

They were only a block and a half from Baked Pizzeria. Still, Lucas managed to make her laugh so much in that short distance that her sides hurt.

She enjoyed his humor as much as she enjoyed seeing

the heat fill his eyes when she flirted with him. She wondered if she was looking at him like that too whenever he leaned close, lowered his voice, and said nice things to her.

She'd never felt so much for someone so quickly. That thought sort of scared her. Falling for someone so fast. Was it possible? After all, she'd been searching for love her entire life.

Chapter Four

There was so much Lucas wanted to tell Avery. So many things about his life—the stories, the happiness, the darkness, everything. He wanted—no, needed—her to understand him better. And he wanted to know everything about her.

Still, he doubted that a crowded pizza place, with them covered in a layer of dust, was the best place or time to get to know one another further.

After they finished their pizza, he walked her to her car and then walked back into his place.

Stepping into the dark building, he still had a smile on his face, and the enormous list of items that still had to be done no longer weighed as heavily on him as it had earlier that day.

As he headed up the stairway that led to the upstairs apartment, he was thankful that he'd at least managed to get the shower upstairs working.

Since he'd moved into the apartment full-time, he hadn't had any time to unpack. His furniture and his motorcycle, an old Harley he'd refurbished, were still sitting in the storage unit in Edgeview until the majority of the remodeling was done.

His mattress sat on the hardwood floor with a stool next to it on one side and a box on the other that he used as his nightstand.

Standing there with a towel wrapped around his hips, he realized just what a disaster it would have been if he'd invited Avery upstairs.

He pulled on some shorts and went to work trying to make the apartment a little cozier. Thankfully, he'd brought his kitchen table and chairs with him on that first trip.

The living room was a little more put together by the time he crawled into bed. His back hurt from the work, but he knew that it would all be worth it. Soon, he was going to have his very own business.

The years of scrimping, working extra shifts, and saving would pay off. Soon.

Early the next morning, he woke to his phone buzzing with a message that his mother, sister, and grandpa were on their way.

By the time they stepped through the front door, he had grabbed a large box of sweets and a few cups of coffee from the bakery down the street.

While his sister chatted about school, friends, and her life, his grandfather added a few other ideas to the growing list of potential names.

Sophia had chopped her hair into a stylish bob a few years back. The style suited her. As did the streak of bright blue that ran through her bangs. She'd pierced her nose a few weeks back and was wearing Doc Martins with checkered pants. Her style was unique. He'd never been popular in school, but Sophia was the most popular kid in her class.

He was just about to tell his family that Avery was

going to stop by and help them that day when she walked through the front door.

Part of him was thankful he hadn't mentioned her to his family beforehand. He hated getting teased by them about a woman he liked. Besides, he liked seeing their genuine first impressions of her on their faces.

After quick introductions, they split into three groups. His grandfather and Avery prepped the walls in the main room for painting. His mother and sister cleaned the kitchens, while he headed over to the local hardware store to pick up the large sander he'd rented to strip the floors.

When he returned, it was to laughter. He'd seen Parker's truck in front of the store and knew that he and his crew were working on the roof and in the basement on the plumbing and electricity already.

His mother and sister almost had the kitchen cleared of all clutter and trash so he could start deep cleaning in there soon.

He hauled the sander in and set it in the middle of the floor. "So," he asked Avery, "you've done this before?"

She smiled and nodded. "With this exact machine. About two years back." She walked over and tapped the handle. "Do you have masks? It's going to get dusty in here."

He nodded. "They're upstairs. We can start after lunch, once my family leaves. Until then, why don't we all head to the kitchen to start deep cleaning?"

Everyone piled into the massive kitchen, which was almost twice the size of the rest of the space. The appliances would be replaced soon. He'd ordered them from a local store in Edgeview two days before. They would take a few days to get there, which would hopefully give him enough time to have everything ready.

The floors in the kitchen were old, cracked, brown tiles

that he hoped to replace. Later. When his budget allowed for it.

After the down payment on the building, the new appliances, new booths, paint, fixtures, and all the repairs that Parker and his crew had to do, he had just enough to hire a kitchen crew and waitstaff, get supplies, and open for business. The money he'd make on Hannah and Wyatt's wedding would help stretch his budget.

If everything went as planned, maybe he could spend that extra money on remodeling the patio area.

The five of them worked in the kitchen until it was cleaner than the last kitchen that he'd worked in. Then everyone headed over to the Golden Oar for burgers.

"I like her," his grandfather said softly while Avery chatted with his sister.

"Who?" he joked, earning a nudge from him.

"Is she the reason you chose Pride?" he asked.

Lucas glanced over at Avery. "No, just a bonus." He watched Avery laugh at something his sister said.

The pair of them had their heads bent over his sister's phone. When Avery glanced up at him with a grin on her lips, he frowned.

"What is she showing you?" He reached for his sister's phone and gasped at the image of him at twelve, holding Sophia, who was a toddler at the time, with chocolate cake all over his head.

Then, seeing the happiness on both his and his sister's faces, he laughed.

"That's a stupid picture." He handed his sister's phone back.

"You're stupid." Sophia stuck her tongue out at him and then went back to showing Avery pictures. Thankfully, they were images of the family cats dressed up as pumpkins the previous Halloween.

"Well, we'd better head back. I have work," his mother said when everyone was finished eating their lunch.

He and Avery walked his family out to their car. He kissed his mother's cheek and hugged his grandpa and sister.

"I like your family," Avery said as he drove them back to his place.

"They seem to like you. Then again, my sister can get along with anyone." He laughed. "She's the most popular kid in school."

"I figured. I was pretty popular as well." Avery beamed.

"I can see that about you." He glanced at her as he parked in front of the building.

"What about you?" Avery asked as he turned off the car.

"Nope, I was a geek. I was below a geek. A nerd." He laughed when she gasped.

"I can't see that." She shook her head. "No one who looks the way you do could be a nerd."

"You saw pictures of when I was a teenager. I weighed one-twenty, soaking wet." He smiled. "Had acne, spent more time in cooking classes than the gym, and worked a nighttime job at a Chinese restaurant instead of playing sports. I was also helping raise my much younger sister, so my studies suffered." He shifted towards her.

"You didn't play any sports?" she asked.

He shook his head. "Not during school. I picked up basketball and football later." He smiled, remembering the football game they'd played on the beach. "I'm not as skilled as you are, but I can toss a ball without embarrassing myself."

She chuckled, and the rich sound warmed him and had his smile growing.

"You did pretty well. No one is as good as I am," she joked. "I wanted to play in high school."

"Why didn't you?"

She shook her head. "Let's just say that the coach was too old-fashioned to allow it, even after everyone fought for my spot on the team." She shrugged. "It ruined it for me. I don't like being where I'm not wanted."

His eyebrows shot up. "I think it would make me fight even harder to prove that I had a right to be there."

"By the time the coach relented, it was baseball season. The next year I wasn't into it that much." She looked at his store. "I suppose my entire life I've been searching for what I want. Where I fit in. It's probably the main reason I have half a dozen jobs at the moment."

"Really? Half a dozen?" To his surprise, she rattled off six or seven business names in Pride.

"You must have a ton of skills," he thought aloud.

She laughed. "That's what you took away from that?"

Smiling, he turned fully towards her. "So quit." She laughed even harder at him. "Do it. Come work for me, full time."

She stopped laughing. "Doing what?"

"Business manager. I'm going to be busy in the kitchen. You've worked at all the top restaurants in town. You must know how to hire, fire, train employees, market, and run a business by now. So come do it for me. Full time. One job. No more running around."

"Don't you want to do that yourself?"

He laughed. "Honestly, when thinking about starting my restaurant, it's the one thing I *didn't* want to do." He held up his hands in a pleading gesture. "Don't make me beg."

Her eyes narrowed. "What if I'm terrible?"

"Then you can fire yourself," he said with a smile. When she shook her head, he sighed and thought quickly. "Okay, how about a trial basis? We can reassess things six months after opening the doors."

"Six months can make or break a business. How about three months?" she said after a moment.

"Deal." He held out his hand for her, eager to get her to agree with the plan.

When she placed her smaller hand in his, he held back a cheer as they shook on it.

"Now, how about we head back and start working on that floor?" she suggested. "I'm dying to see what's underneath all that black stain." She clapped her hands. "After I make a few calls so I can continue working here," she added as she got out of his car.

He did a little fist-in-the-air motion as a celebration and then followed her into the building.

Okay, so she was a million times better at using the sander than he was. The thing had a mind of its own and kept pulling to one side when he was in control. When she did it, it looked effortless.

So while she slowly glided over every inch of the hardwood flooring, he got busy removing the old wood paneling in the back hallway.

When Parker and his crew returned from lunch, they headed up to the rooftop.

He'd talked to Parker earlier that morning and agreed to the patches and repairs they were doing on the flat roof. They were supposed to get rain later that week, so the roof was the highest priority.

After they were done with that, there were a ton of electric and plumbing fixes in the basement.

He'd just finished removing and hauling all the old dark paneling to the dumpster when he heard the sander shut off.

Stepping into the room, he held in a slight gasp.

Avery was standing in front of the front windows. The light from the sunset was streaming in, making her vibrant red hair glow like a halo around her face.

Her beauty quite literally took his breath away.

Without thinking, he stepped towards her, lifted his hand to her face, and slowly leaned closer. She could have pulled away. Could have told him to piss off. Instead, the slightest curve of her lips invited him further.

When their lips brushed, something rushed through him, a zap of awareness he'd never felt before in his entire life. He could never have imagined he would ever feel something so powerful.

For the first time in his life, he was awake in every aspect. He had total awareness. All of his senses were on fire. Everything converged to this one moment.

"Wow," Avery said against his lips.

"Yeah, wow." He rested his forehead against hers.

Just then they both heard Parker's crew heading down the stairs. He took a giant step back as the workers stepped into the room.

"Wow, this looks much better," Parker said with a grin. "So, Sara heard through the grapevine that you're going to be working here full time," Parker said to Avery.

"Yup, just made it official. I still have to tell my dad that I won't be filling in at the station, but I'm sure he's going to be excited." Avery glanced back at him.

"You'll both be happy to know that as of right now, your

roof won't be an issue. We just finished there," Parker said as his workers hauled their tools outside to their trucks. "We will continue working on plumbing and wiring tomorrow. I can't promise that will take a single day." He shook Lucas's hand. "See you in the morning."

"This looks amazing," she said once they were alone. "Better than my parents' flooring." She turned towards him. "Are you going to stain it light or dark?"

"Light," he answered quickly. "I'm thinking of just sealing it."

She nodded. "Good idea."

"We'll need to talk about that kiss," he said suddenly.

He watched her smile slip a little. "I don't want to complicate this. I just agreed to work for you. I don't think it would be wise if we let this"—she motioned between them—"gunk things up."

He felt a slight stab in his chest. Shit. He hadn't thought about it like that. He nodded. "You're right. So we won't mix the two." His heart sank. He took a step closer to her. "I think we both felt a big enough punch with that kiss that we know that it's going to be hard dancing around whatever is between us. I'd like to explore it further, but if it's between you not working here or us enjoying each other, then I can push my feelings aside. For now."

She nodded slowly and he took a step back. "I'll see you tomorrow." She gathered up her bag and headed out the front door. Even the dying sunlight turned her hair a vibrant color. He could still see it when he closed his eyes.

Chapter Five

"What have you done?" Avery's brother stood over her while she devoured a frozen meal in their parents' kitchen.

"I've quit my jobs. All of them," she said with her mouth full.

"Yeah, the entire town is talking about it. Why?" He crossed his arms over his chest.

"What does it matter to you?" she asked, not sparing him a glance. Instead, she scrolled through the dozen or so messages from Hannah, basically asking the same thing.

"Because I finally found a job that I like more than the others," she answered and typed the same thing to Hannah.

"You're serious about this then?" Wyatt sat next to her and reached over to take a tater tot from her plate. She slapped his hand away.

"Get your own." She scooted her plate away from him. If she let him eat one, he'd devour the entire thing. "Yes, I'm serious. So serious that I quite half a dozen jobs today." She smiled up at him.

Wyatt's eyes narrowed. "Is it that guy?"

Avery's eyes narrowed as well. "That guy? Lucas?" She shook her head; the truth was that he was only half of the reason. She was tired of running around town. Tired of working dead-end jobs and never going anywhere.

The chance to manage a brand-new business, one that she had no doubt would be a success with her help, thrilled her. For the first time in years, she was excited about her future.

"Don't mess with me," she warned Wyatt. "All those years I tried to convince you not to be an ass with Hannah." She rolled her eyes.

Her brother's attitude suddenly changed. He leaned back in the chair and was quiet for a moment.

"Fine." Wyatt threw up his hands. "Fine. Don't come crying to me if things don't work out."

"Don't worry, I won't. That's the job of my best friend that you're marrying." She smiled when Hannah replied to her text message with positivity. "See, your soon-to-be wife thinks it's a great idea."

Wyatt sighed loudly. "Where are Mom and Dad this week?"

"Hawaii," she answered. "You know, I think they travel so much just so we come home once and a while."

"They hated it when we moved out," Wyatt agreed.

"They're proud of you though. Coming home. Taking over the grocery store. Finally coming to your senses with Hannah." She nudged his elbow with hers.

"They're proud of you too."

She shook her head. "They'll be prouder of me now that I've finally settled on one job." She beamed. "You should be happy for me too."

"You haven't told them yet?"

She shook her head. "Not yet. I will. When they get back."

Wyatt stood up. "I'm going to head home. For what it's worth, I am proud of you. Just... it's my job to protect you too."

"Remember, I am older than you, which would mean it's my job to protect you."

"Older, but I'm still your big brother." He smiled.

"Size doesn't matter." Avery rolled her eyes and then stuck her tongue out at her brother. "Go home. Hannah's waiting. She says she cooked you some dinner."

Wyatt groaned and Avery laughed, pulling her plate of tater tots away from him once more.

"I'm telling her you groaned," she called after him while typing on her phone.

Staying at her parents' place wasn't all that bad. The guest room used to be her room and was cozy. Still, she missed the beach. She'd gotten spoiled living in the small cottage right off the sand.

Here, her morning jogs were cut short thanks to the highway and lack of road. Down by the beach, she could choose to run on the wet sand or through the town.

Renting the smaller place from Brook was the best thing she could have done for herself. Brook wasn't using it any longer now that she'd married Ryder and they'd moved into the old place on Ocean View. They had just finished renovating the massive house.

So many of her friends had gotten married in the past few years or were about to get married. Honestly, in the past ten years, the little town of Pride has seen more weddings and births than Avery could count.

It was difficult not to be a little jealous or to feel left out. Sure, she'd dated a few times since high school, guys that she'd gone to school with or friends of friends. None of them had led to a second date.

She'd had two somewhat serious boyfriends in high school. Both of them had quickly left Pride after graduation and hadn't returned. She hadn't lost her heart to either of them.

She'd thought about leaving Pride before but she always came to her senses. This was home. It would always be home. She dreamed of finding love and raising her own family here, surrounded by the people she loved and who, without a doubt, loved her back.

One thing was clear to her after working at almost every business in town—there wasn't a person living within the town's borders who wouldn't drop everything to help someone else.

She cleaned up her parents' kitchen and let out her parents' new dog, Blossom. They'd grabbed an older dog from Carrie's Sanctuary shortly after the holidays. Then she headed upstairs

Avery could hardly remember a time when there hadn't been a dog or two in the house. She was thankful Blossom was a few years old and not a puppy. She knew what her brother was going through right now with his new puppy. The chewed-on shoes, the mess on the rugs, and all that energy. Not that she didn't love puppies. When she had her own home and more time, she planned to get one herself.

She should have been exhausted after all the back-breaking work she'd done that day, but she lay in bed and stared at the ceiling, thinking and worrying about what she'd just done. For the first time in years, she was going to focus on one job.

Would she grow bored of it?

She knew part of the reason she bounced around all the

time was because she often grew tired of working on the same tasks over and over. Blame it on her ADHD or the fact that she thrived on new adventures.

Had she made the right choice? Could she settle down?

Then the memory of Lucas kissing her replayed in her head and she smiled as she finally drifted off to sleep.

The following morning she held a box of breakfast sandwiches and coffee as Lucas pushed the door open for her.

"Morning," she beamed as he took the items from her.

"Morning." He shifted and took the offered cup of coffee.

"I didn't know how you would like your coffee so I just ordered two of my favorite. Caramel latte." She set her bag behind the countertop as he set their food down.

"That's my favorite as well." He smiled. "You didn't have to get breakfast. I figured we'd walk over after you got here."

"It's okay. I had to swing by there and pick up my last check." She pulled out a breakfast sandwich and handed it to Lucas.

He frowned. "I promise this will be worth it."

She chuckled. "If I didn't think that, I wouldn't be here." She held up her cup. "To new beginnings." He smiled and tapped his cup to hers.

They worked on finishing the kitchen. Since Parker and his guys would be in the basement for the foreseeable future, they decided to hold off on staining and sealing the floor until they could be sure that no one would walk on it.

They tackled the huge freezer, which had mold inside it. They cleaned, scrubbed, and sanitized every inch of the massive thing. In the end, they decided that the old shelving had to be pulled out and hosed off in the alley. That made the process go more quickly.

She felt and looked like someone in a science-fiction flick, covered in latex from head to toe with the heavy ventilator on and gloves that reached her elbows.

It was the least sexy outfit she'd ever worn. Still, she and Lucas joked with one another and laughed more than she had on any date she'd gone on.

By the end of the day, she desperately needed to clean off and spent an extra half hour enjoying the hot spray in her parents' large shower.

The following day, they worked on the bathrooms. She spent almost half the day scrubbing the white tile floors in both small bathrooms.

After lunch, he suggested she start working on the office at the end of the hallway by the staircase. The room was roughly the same size as one of the two bathrooms across the hallway. There was an older desk and chair in it and a filing cabinet that she'd already cleared out. When she suggested to Lucas that they paint the walls in the room, he agreed and told her that she could pick the color of the walls.

She was halfway through cleaning out the old desk when he popped his head in and mentioned that this would be her office. After Lucas disappeared again, she let out a gleeful sound and returned to the task with extra vigor. This was going to be her office.

She'd assumed that he would be the one inhabiting the space. After all, he was the owner. It did make sense as his business manager that she'd have a desk. She'd just never assumed she'd have an entire office. In all the jobs she'd had before, she'd never had an office to herself.

When the room was spotless, she took a few moments to move the desk around, giving the room a bigger feeling than before. Now, if she wanted, she could have a small sofa or two chairs facing the desk.

Lucas poked his head in again. "Nice. The room looks twice the size now."

"Just wait until I paint the walls. This dirty dark brown makes it feel as if the walls are closing in on you." She dusted off her hands. "Are you sure you won't need this space? You are the owner of the restaurant."

He shook his head. "I have an office upstairs if I need one. There's also a small room off the kitchen I plan to use."

"Oh, right, I'd forgotten that there's an upstairs." She glanced up to the ceiling. "You have an apartment up there too?"

He nodded. "I'd invite you up, but there's a lot of work I still need to do before I have company."

"Once we're done down here, I could always help up there," she suggested.

"Maybe when I paint the walls. For now, down here is what matters the most."

She'd never seen the apartment upstairs. When she worked at the sandwich shop in high school, the owner had lived up there. She wanted to see what it was like but knew better than to push.

"I can bring my laptop to use for now," she told me.

"No, don't bother. My cousin has set me up with Josh. He'll be here next week to set up the point-of-sale system and a computer in here and one upstairs for my use." He leaned against the door frame. "You need a sofa or chairs right there." He motioned to the spot she'd left empty for that purpose.

"Yes, I was going to check with Lilly to see if she has a couple of chairs or head over to Ruby's Antiques. I think a standard-sized sofa would be too big."

He nodded. "We can maybe head over to Classy and

Sassy tomorrow sometime. They were holding some mirrors for the bathroom for me."

She liked that he was shopping locally for the place. It was important and would no doubt reflect well on him as a business owner to everyone in town.

She planned to do most of the purchasing for the restaurant locally as well. Most everyone she'd worked for thus far used local first.

"I suppose we need to talk about a few details. Stocking, supplies, hiring, that sort of thing," she said.

He nodded. "We have time." He glanced at his watch. "But we can head over and grab a pizza and knock out a few items if you want?"

"Sure." She stood up and dusted herself off, then grabbed her bag. "You live upstairs?" she asked as they walked through the light rain to Baked.

"Yup. Are you in town?" he asked, glancing at her.

"Normally, I live in a cottage on the beach not far from the public beach area. However, this week, my parents are in Hawaii, and I'm house- and dog-sitting for them. They live up there." She motioned to the hillside that overlooked the town. On a clear day, you could see her parents' roof from there. Today, the clouds clung to the hillside, blocking their view.

"My mother is a cat person," he told her.

She laughed. "Yes, your sister had a million photos of them. She tells me they're social media famous."

He rolled his eyes and chuckled. "My sister dresses them up and makes them act out famous movies or scenes."

"I know, I started following them. The Romeo and Juliet death scene was hilarious."

He laughed as he held the door open for her. "Okay, she has a talent for putting a scene together. Wait until you watch the *Titanic* scene." He leaned a little closer and whispered. "Here's a hint. Jack doesn't make it onto the door."

She laughed as she spotted her brother and Hannah across the room. Waving at them, she followed Lucas to the counter.

"Since your brother and Hannah are here," Lucas said as they waited, "want to sit with them?"

"Sure," she said, wishing more than anything for more time alone with him. But she figured they'd have plenty of time alone since they still had a lot of work to do on the place before opening day.

Chapter Six

One thing was clear after eating lunch at the same table as Avery's brother and soon-to-be sister-in-law. The three of them were very close. So close that they finished each other's sentences.

He didn't have any friends that close. He'd had a few friends in school but they had gone separate ways after graduation. Mark was in the military and stationed somewhere overseas, and Curt was married with three kids, living in California.

He hadn't realized he'd been missing the company of good friends until he'd watched the three of them laughing and joking with one another. So when Wyatt asked him to join him and a few others once a week to play basketball at the gym, he'd jumped at the chance.

"I'll warn you, I'm not very good," he told Wyatt.

"None of us are," Wyatt said as he leaned back and wrapped his arm around Hannah.

Thankfully, during the meal, they'd talked about menu items for their wedding, and he was able to get some idea of what they wanted for their big day.

He hadn't known if they were shooting for a fancy wedding or something more down to earth. The way they talked, they were smack in the middle of the two, and he could think of two dozen items that would fit perfectly for the event.

He planned to hit up his local contacts to get his cousins' place stocked with everything that he would need first thing the next day.

By the time everyone walked out of the restaurant together, he had a better feel for the couple and had narrowed down what he would make to eight different options.

"You got quiet," Avery said when they stood in the parking lot, watching the other couple leave.

He rattled off the list of dishes that he planned to make for the couple.

Avery's eyes grew wide and then she was smiling. "I can't wait to taste it all."

"Do you think they'll enjoy it?" He motioned with his head to where her brother's car had disappeared.

"Without a doubt. Are you worried? Because I can assure you, you shouldn't be." She crossed her arms over her chest as a gust of wind hit them. He took her arm and led her back down the street quickly.

"Your brother holds a lot of weight around town, being the owner of the grocery store. Not to mention all the people Hannah deals with daily. If they don't like my food, then I fear my restaurant won't stand a chance in hell," he said in one long breath.

"Lucas." She touched his arm. "Trust me when I say that my brother and Hannah are not food snobs. I've tasted your cooking and, whatever you make, they're going to love it."

He relaxed a little. "I might feel better if I had a dry run before this weekend," he murmured.

"Okay, then cook two of the dishes for me. The beef carnitas and sopes sound amazing."

He was frowning. "I don't have a working kitchen."

"There's one at my parents' place." She smiled. "Tomorrow after we're done working, we can grab what you need at the store, then head on up to their place."

It wasn't until later that day, when he was watching Avery's taillights leave after they finished cleaning the freezer and refrigerator, that he realized he'd just agreed to have a private dinner with her. Did she think of it as a date?

They'd agreed to keep things casual. Right?

While he headed upstairs to shower, he replayed in his head what she had said after the kiss.

"I don't want to complicate this. I just agreed to work for you. I don't think it would be wise if we let this gunk things up."

He'd been a fool at the moment and had agreed with her. But neither of them had officially said that a physical relationship was off-limits. Had they?

Damn. Now he was second-guessing this.

After his shower, he jotted down the possible menu that he was thinking of for Wyatt and Hannah's big day. Then in clear rows under each dish's heading, he listed each item that he'd need to make it.

By the time he fell into bed, at least those worries were no longer circling through his head. Still, the memory of Avery's lips pressed against his kept him tossing and turning for the rest of the night.

He overslept the next morning and had to rush downstairs to let Parker and his crew inside. By the time Avery arrived, he was covered in a layer of dust and soaking wet from helping Parker out in the basement with a busted pipe.

"What did you do? Fall into a well?" Avery asked with a chuckle.

"If I had, I don't think I would have gotten as wet. A pipe in the basement decided to bust in two." He rolled his eyes. "Parker and his crew are replacing it and a bunch of other ones right now."

She ran her eyes up and down him, and he suddenly realized the white shirt he was wearing was sticking to his skin. He quickly pulled it away from his chest. "I'm going to head upstairs and change into dry clothes." He started walking towards the stairs. His shoes squeaked with each step he took, causing Avery to laugh.

"You might need dry shoes while you're at it," she called after him.

He nodded and caught himself from slipping on the wet floor from the water he'd just dripped all over the place. He grabbed a hand towel and tossed it on the floor.

"I'll mop that up. Go on up and change." Avery rushed over to him with a mop in hand.

She didn't see his wet footprints on the floor and started slipping as she let out a soft cry of distress.

He was by her side quickly, wrapping his arms around her to keep her from falling to the floor and hurting herself.

Her body pressed tight against his chest. Her hands were trapped between them, still holding the mop tightly.

"Are you okay?" he asked her, not chancing releasing her in case she didn't have her footing yet.

"Yes." She chuckled. "Now I'm soaked too." She glanced down between them.

Seeing that he was indeed getting her shirt wet, he released her and almost ended up on the floor himself.

"Okay, we need a wet floor sign," he mumbled. "Maybe a runner down this hallway where the tile starts."

"I'll add it to my growing list." She held onto the wall and moved slowly as she mopped the floor.

"Sorry," he added. "About getting you wet."

She shrugged. "I wore my work shirt today. I had plans to clear up the outside patio area since it's nice out."

"Great idea. I'll be right out to help you. After I change." He disappeared upstairs.

When he finally made it outside, she had two trash bags full already. The alley, or patio area as she was currently calling it, had many years' worth of debris lying around.

It took them almost two hours to clear the space of all the trash that had blown into the alleyway.

While he used a shovel to scoop up the excess dirt and sand from what appeared to be large pavers on the ground, Avery swept the door stoop and pathway areas clear.

By lunchtime, the entire patio was ready to be decorated.

"This turned out better than I thought it would," he admitted. "I think there's enough room for at least eight small tables out here if we stick to two seats at each."

"How about six two-seaters and one that seats four?" she suggested. "Plus a row of planters here," She motioned. "To put a small separation between the street and the diners."

"With string lights going between the buildings." He glanced up. "Oh, I have a balcony." He frowned up at the rod iron thing hanging off his living room window. He hadn't noticed it before.

She moved over beside him and glanced up. "You haven't noticed that before now?"

He shook his head. "I've been too preoccupied with the

downstairs to notice. There's a whole other room I haven't even looked in yet. I had planned to use it as a storage area."

"How could you not explore every inch after you got the keys?" she asked in an excited tone as she continued looking at the building.

Her arm brushed up against him, sending an instant wave of awareness and heat through him. He could smell the soft floral scent she wore as the summer breeze floated over them.

His mind turned towards her, consumed by everything she was. If he had the keys to unlock the mysteries that she held, he would take his time learning every inch of her.

Just then Parker opened the door. "There you are," Parker said. "Oh, hey, Avery."

"Hi, Parker," Avery said cheerfully as she stepped away from Lucas.

"We could use your help again," Parker said to him.

"Sure thing." He turned to go.

"I can head over to the deli at O'Neil's and grab us some sandwiches if you want?" Avery suggested. "For your guys too?"

"Sounds good. We're going to be stuck in the basement for a while," Parker said. "You can come get the orders from the others if you want. We have most of the water pumped out of the basement."

Avery nodded and then followed them to the basement.

Parker was right. There were small puddles of water in places now instead of the inch or two that had been down there earlier.

He was thankful they'd shut off the loud pump so the entire building was no longer vibrating. While Avery took everyone's sandwich orders, he answered a few questions that Parker had about the electricity and plumbing.

When he'd purchased the building, he'd been surprised at how spacious the basement was. There was a large storeroom in which he planned to put shelves for beer and wine storage. Since it was directly under where he planned to put the fountain drink dispenser, he was having Parker run the lines for the canisters, which is what Parker had questions about.

While they figured out the best place for everything, his men continued working on replacing the old plumbing for the water heater and kitchen areas.

When Avery returned, loaded with sandwiches, they all sat around and ate on the newly cleaned patio area.

He was very entertained watching the way Avery interacted with everyone and wondered if there was anyone in town whose life story she didn't know.

He'd been born in Edgeview and had lived there his entire life and still only knew a handful of people in the larger town. He doubted he could recall any of their lives or family names like Avery could for each of the workers.

When Parker and his men returned inside, he and Avery stayed outside for a few more minutes.

"It must have been nice growing up in Pride," he said, leaning back against the wall.

"It was." She smiled and leaned back as well. "Still is." She laughed. "I'm only twenty-six. My grandparents would say I have a lot more growing up to do."

He chuckled when he remembered his grand-pap saying something similar. "I bet there isn't one person in town you don't know everything about."

She frowned as she thought about it. "There are a lot of people, I'd wager. After all, the Coast Guard training center has a lot of turnover."

"Right. I mean the real locals. The ones that stick."

She sighed and rested her head back against the brick wall. "Some like my brother tried not to stick. When he left, everyone wondered if he'd ever return. They were pretty sure he'd gotten city fever."

"City... fever?"

"Sure, you know, getting spoiled by being able to order Uber Eats or Grubhub. Being able to go to many different stores if you don't find what you want. Movie theaters."

"We have a movie theater, just back that way." He pointed.

She chuckled. "That runs two movies at a time."

"Edgeview is only twenty minutes away."

"When there's two feet of snow on the ground, twenty minutes can turn into an hour."

"Right." He nodded. "Still, it's better than not having the option. Did you ever want to move to the city?" he asked her.

"Never," she answered quickly. "You?"

"I'm from a city," he joked. "Growing up, that's what I thought Edgeview was."

"Now?" she asked.

"Now it just seems too crowded with people I don't know or care to know. People too busy to stop and have a chat or a good meal."

She was quiet as she watched him. "You're not going to open a hugely successful business here, then go off and franchise it all over the world?"

He laughed. "Nope, I'm going to be very content just having one successful business for the rest of my life in a town where everyone knows everyone else's life stories."

Chapter Seven

Avery was getting very excited about having Lucas come over and make her dinner. Earlier that morning, she'd made sure that her parents' place was spotless for the evening. Not that the home wasn't always spotless, but she made sure to do some extra cleaning in the kitchen in preparation.

Lucas was going to stop by the grocery store one last time on his way up to the house, which gave her a little time to let Blossom out and play with her in the yard.

They were still outside enjoying the dying sunlight when Lucas drove up and parked beside her car.

Most people who saw her parents' house for the first time had the same look on their faces. From the driveway, her childhood home was, well, charming.

Sure, it was a standard four-bedroom, three-bath, two-car garage home like many other homes scattered through the countryside surrounding Pride.

But from the front, the home looked massive with three balconies, a wraparound deck, and a huge garage that her father also used as a workshop.

"Hello, who is this?" Lucas bent down and gave Blossom his attention when the dog dropped her ball at his feet.

"My parents' latest spoiled animal. Lucas, this is Blossom."

The dog sat down on her butt and lifted a paw towards Lucas, who laughed as he shook it. "Nice to meet you."

"Can we help you bring everything in?" she offered.

"Sure." He turned back to his car and handed her a paper bag full of fresh vegetables. "I'll get the rest," he said as he grabbed the other two bags.

She led them into the house, making sure that Blossom followed before walking through to the kitchen in the back.

"You grew up here?" Lucas asked as they set the bags down on the countertop.

"I was born right over there." She pointed to the fireplace. "One winter night when they were snowed in."

"Seriously?" Lucas focused on the fireplace. "Not in a hospital? That must have freaked your parents out."

"My dad is a fireman." She chuckled. "But honestly, my mother did all the work."

"That's incredible. I'd love to hear the whole story," he said as he started to remove each of the items from the bags.

She started telling him the story of her birth while helping him figure out where everything was in her parents' kitchen. Then she sat back and watched him work.

He moved like so many other chefs she'd seen before. He was smooth, almost as if it were all a dance.

She liked to cook and knew the basics. There were at least a dozen decent meals she could get through without having to look at a recipe book and at least twice that number for baked goods. If she had to choose, she'd rather bake than cook. Still, Lucas made it look so easy.

"Wine?" he said, setting a glass in front of her while she told him about how her parents were thrilled to learn they were expecting Wyatt a few short months after her birth.

"Thanks," she said and took a sip. Then she stilled and took another sip. "What is this?" She frowned down at the glass.

Lucas chuckled. "Wine."

"No, it's... spicy. I like it." She took another sip.

"It has jalapeños in it." He turned the label to her. "I plan to offer it in the restaurant. It's from Regal Wineries. They're a local winery, sort of. They are on the south side of Edgeview." He went back to work.

She took another sip of the wine. It was sweet yet had a zippy aftertaste. She enjoyed it.

"It must have been nice growing up with a sibling close to your age. I can remember the day Sophia was born perfectly." He smiled over his shoulder at her.

Gosh, he was dreamy when he smiled. She leaned her elbow on the countertop as she sipped her wine and just watched him for a few minutes while he talked about the day his younger sister was born.

She wondered if he even had to think as he chopped the vegetables. His hands moved so fluidly and quickly. She knew without a doubt she would have cut herself more than once at that speed.

By the time the smell of the rich food filled the entire house, she was starved. For both the food and the man.

She'd never really found guys wearing an apron sexy before, but Lucas pulled the look off very well.

Thankfully, she'd set out her parents' good dishes and had cleared the table of her normal clutter. Now, there were only her mother's new honey candlesticks in the stone holders she'd bought one Mother's Day along with the vase of fresh wildflowers that she'd picked the evening before on her walk with the dog.

After Lucas set several dishes full of colorful food down, he held out a chair for her.

"This all looks so amazing. I have no idea where to start," she said as she sat.

Instead of sitting down beside her, he motioned to each dish as he called out the names and gave a short explanation of each.

She smiled when she noticed that his accent got thicker when he talked about the food.

Some dishes she knew, such as the beef carnitas and sopes. The others she wasn't familiar with, but she could tell that she was going to enjoy them, no matter their names.

At his suggestion, she tried the stuffed poblanos first, followed by a sampling of both beef and chicken tinga. By the time she dug into the beef birria tacos, she was in love.

"My brother and Hannah are going to love all of this," she said with her mouth full as she took another bite.

"I was thinking of these three dishes, along with either beef albondigas or pork verde as the soup," Lucas said, finally sitting down and taking one of the birria tacos.

"All of it," she said, "Of course, Hannah has already planned for an open margarita bar." She finished off one of the tingas and grabbed another one. "You're going to cook all of this for us again this weekend?"

He nodded as he took a sip of his beer.

She took a moment, what felt like her first since sitting down to eat, to breathe and take a sip of her wine.

"I'll have time to prepare the soups. The verde takes several hours to slow cook." He smiled and then motioned. "I didn't bake anything, but this weekend I was thinking of having both tres leches and my take on the classic churros. I know they'll have a wedding cake, but it might be nice to have smaller sampler-style desserts. I was going to suggest the idea to them this weekend."

"I love it." She set her wine glass down. "The last wedding I attended, there was a long line for the cake and by the time I got there, the chocolate cake was all gone. I had to settle for yellow cake." She rolled her eyes, causing Lucas to chuckle.

"Chocolate is my favorite too." He picked up another taco.

"When did you decide you wanted to be a chef?" she asked, returning to her food.

She watched his smile slip a little.

"I was about eight. My mother had... broken her arm and couldn't make me dinner. She was laid up in bed and told me I could go into the kitchen and make myself a peanut butter and jelly sandwich. Instead, I made us chicken tacos like my grandpa had shown me the last time he'd been over at the house. I remember watching him cook and thinking it was magic. Taking all those different things and putting them together to make something so tasty. Every kid can make a peanut butter and jelly sandwich." His smile returned. "Not every kid can make my grandpa's tacos. My mother was so impressed that I hadn't burned the house down." Avery laughed and Lucas glanced over at her with a smile. "She also thought my tacos were the very best she'd had. Of course, she's my mother and was required to say that."

Avery laughed again. "My mother has never hesitated to tell me just how bad my cooking is."

Lucas laughed. "I'm sure you're good at other things."

Avery's face heated and she reached for her wine as thoughts of being with Lucas filled her mind.

She needed to go out on dates more often. Sure, there was that kiss. Even now her knees went weak at the thought of his lips against hers.

This was her chance to settle herself and her life down. Her first opportunity to prove to herself and everyone else that she could make something of herself. That she wasn't just a feather in the wind, being blown around from job to job.

She wanted this job to last. And flirting with her new boss might just jeopardize that future.

"What about Sophia?" she asked and leaned back in her chair. If she didn't stop eating now, she'd have to unbutton her pants.

Lucas's dark eyebrows rose slowly.

"Does she like cooking as much as you?" she asked.

Lucas shook his head. "Nope, she's really into her cat video thing. She's taking violin lessons from our grandfather, but even that she's already bored with."

Avery smiled. "Did you see the video she did last night?"

Lucas laughed. "Loki and Thor." He rolled his eyes. "I can tell Rusty, which is the orange cat, was not into being dressed as Thor."

"The other one, the black cat," she started.

"Luna."

"It's a girl?" She laughed when he nodded in agreement. "I can tell she wasn't into it either."

"They're getting older and have less patience for my sister's shenanigans." He grinned as he leaned back in his chair and looked around. "How often do you house-sit?"

She shrugged. "More than I used to. My parents are enjoying their empty-nest days."

"I doubt my mother would know what to do with

herself without Sophia in the house. When I moved out, she almost had a breakdown until I pointed out that Sophia was years away from moving out." He started clearing the table. She stood up and helped.

"I can clean—" She stopped when his dark eyebrows shot up slowly.

"A great chef never leaves others to clean up after him or her." He winked and then took the dishes from her hands. "Besides, you need to sit and enjoy dessert."

"I thought you said you weren't going to make anything?" She sat at the bar top again to watch him clean up.

"I didn't make it myself. Just this one time I bought it. Your brother swore by it though." He pulled a pie from one of the containers he'd brought in earlier and set it in front of her.

She instantly felt her mouth water. "My brother must like you."

"Oh?" Lucas paused as he cut her a slice of the pie. "Why is that?"

"This right there is my all-time favorite pie." She motioned to the French silk pie.

Lucas set a plate with a slice in front of her. "I'll make sure to remember that."

"What's yours?" she asked, picking up her fork and taking a bite. She stilled as the richness and sweetness melted on the tip of her tongue.

When he didn't answer, she glanced up. Lucas was watching her with so much interest that she worried she had some chocolate on her face.

"Whatever makes you moan with pleasure like that is my new favorite anything," he said in a low voice.

Instantly, her insides bubbled and warmed. Thoughts of

wrapping her body around his played in her head. Images of him naked caused her face to heat. Hell, her entire body sizzled.

Then, as if he had just realized what he'd said, he turned around and bumped solidly into the countertop and the moment was over. After catching himself so he didn't fall over, he went back to work cleaning up.

"This isn't going to work, is it?" she asked after a very long moment of silence.

"What?" He frowned over at her.

"Avoiding." She motioned between them with her fork.

He shrugged. "I've worked with plenty of women I was attracted to and kept things professional." He went back to washing her mother's pans. "I'm sure that after we open the doors, we'll have less one-on-one time together." He glanced over his shoulder. "You may come to hate me as a boss and a person."

She laughed. "I doubt that." She leaned slightly towards him. "But is that all we have between us? Just attraction?"

His eyes moved over her face, and he cleared his throat and reached for his drink. "You're making this harder."

She smiled and shrugged. "What's the fun in easy?"

He narrowed his eyes slightly and then turned and went back to work.

She watched his broad shoulders as he worked and wondered just how she was going to keep herself in check around him. Maybe they didn't have to. She was still very friendly with a few of the men she'd dated before. She had even worked with them a few times and did not have any issues.

"Have you ever had a bad breakup?" she asked when he was done cleaning.

"Not really." He stood across from her and cut himself a

slice of pie, then set a much smaller second piece on her plate. "Terra poured a container of milk on my head when she found out I'd talked to her arch nemesis during recess in third grade. By junior high, however, we were friends again," he said between bites. "You?"

She shook her head. "I'm not enemies with any of them."

"Me either. Then again, I haven't seen any of my exes in years. Most of my classmates with a brain moved out of state shortly after graduation."

"You stuck around," she pointed out.

"I had to."

"Your mom?" she asked.

He nodded. "Why did you?"

She didn't have to. She wanted to. She loved Pride. Loved everyone in it.

Would Lucas understand that? Would he think she was strange?

She'd already confided in him that she loved the town. Loved her jobs. Loved the people.

"It's home," she answered casually. At least she hoped it sounded casual.

"In the short time I've spent living here, I can see the charm of sticking around." He finished his pie and took their plates and rinsed them off.

He leaned back on the countertop when he was done. "So, be honest with me."

"About?" She rested her chin in her hands as she leaned on the counter.

"Do you think your brother and Hannah are going to want the beef or the chicken tinga?"

"Both," she chuckled.

He crossed his arms over his chest before nodding.

"Well, I'm just thankful I get to do this all over again in two days."

"I can help," she offered. "Now that I've watched you work, I can at least lend a hand."

He smiled. "I'd like that. When we get closer to opening day, I'm going to have to interview and train a few other kitchen staff." He took a deep breath and then, to her surprise, he started gathering his things.

She wanted to ask him to stay a little longer but knew that if they were going to keep things professional, it would be better for him to leave.

"Thanks for letting me run a few dishes by you first," he said as they walked towards the front door.

"Thanks for the wonderful meal," she countered. "After tonight's sampling, I can guarantee you'll be in business a very long time in Pride."

His smile practically doubled. "Thanks." He held open the door, his arms full of the bags he'd brought with him, which were now empty. "Let me just clear the air on one thing." His eyes searched hers. "I want to kiss you right now. But..."

She didn't know what caused her to rush up on her toes and quickly cover his mouth with hers. Maybe it was because his hands were full and she knew that she'd be in control and able to keep herself in check just as long as he didn't touch her.

"There," she said as she took a step away from him. Just the simple quick contact with his lips had her swaying slightly. "Thank you for dinner." Before he could respond, she shut the door.

Chapter Eight

What in the hell was a guy to do? Avery had knocked him out with that quick kiss the night before and this morning, she was hanging all over another man. He didn't figure he was spying, since she and the other man in question were standing in the middle of the road across from his place. All he had to do was stand by the window of his apartment and look out to see the couple close together with the morning mist swirling around them.

The fog wasn't helping him determine who the other man was. At first, he'd thought it was her brother. Then he'd gotten a better look and knew that it wasn't.

This man was much taller. Broader in the shoulders.

The raincoat that the man had on was doing a great job of hiding his face from Lucas's view.

What he did see was Avery reach up on her toes, hug the man, and kiss him on the cheek. Then she stood in the middle of the empty road and chatted with him as if they had all the time in the world to do so while the rain continued to fall.

When a car finally did pass by, they stepped aside and waved and continued talking as if not bothered by the rain or the distraction.

Who was it? He squinted slightly and made the mistake of moving a little to get a better view. Avery's head jerked towards the building, and he watched her eyes lift towards the window.

Afraid that she'd see him spying on them, he jerked back to get out of the window. Unfortunately, he forgot about the row of boxes behind him and started to trip. Reaching out for anything to stop his fall, he grabbed a handful of curtains and yanked down the shower rod that was holding them up.

The entire thing came crashing down on top of him when he landed on his left hip and elbow.

There was no doubt in his mind that Avery and the mystery man would now know he'd been spying on them. His living room lights were on and they could now get a full view of his brightly lit rooms.

Groaning, he decided to lie on the floor for a few moments until Avery let herself in downstairs. Then he'd try to avoid her for the rest of the day so he didn't die of embarrassment.

Unfortunately, since they were the only two people in the building for the day, that was impossible.

Almost an hour later, he stood back as a truck of furniture was unloaded. His new tables and chairs—new to him at any rate—were hauled into the basement.

Once the crew was done unloading everything, he and Avery started working to finally seal the wood floors.

By the time the sun had set, they had finished with the first coat. He was very thankful that Avery knew what she was doing since he had no clue. It had taken a lot longer than anticipated since several boards had needed repair first.

"What time are you going to get to your cousins' place tomorrow and when do you want me there?" she asked as she slipped on her rain jacket to go.

"I plan to serve them around five, so I'll want to get there a couple of hours earlier. Since we can't walk on the floor until the day after tomorrow, there's no use in you coming in in the morning. If you want to help out, you can head over to my cousins' place around three?"

She nodded and smiled. "You don't need any help shopping for everything?"

He shook his head. "No, I've got that handled." He glanced at the floor one last time and smiled. "It sure looks great."

"Think of how wonderful it will look after the second coat and the sealer." She zipped up her coat and pulled on her hood. They could hear the rain coming down even harder outside.

"Are you sure you want to go out in that right now?" He nodded towards the back door, which they had left open while they were working to get fresh air circulating in the room.

She chuckled. "We live in Oregon. This is nothing." She shifted slightly and glanced towards the door to the stairs that led up to his apartment. "How are you doing up there?"

He held in a groan of disappointment. "Not as good as down here. But I hadn't planned to do much work on the apartment until after we opened the doors."

"I could help?" she offered.

He shook his head. "I couldn't ask you, nor do I want

you to see the mess that I'm living in right now." He chuckled. "You'll have to trust me that I'm a neat freak."

Suddenly she got a funny smile on her lips. "Did you hang up your curtains again?"

He groaned and closed his eyes.

"Just so we're clear, that was my friend Brook's husband, Ryder, I ran into this morning. He and Brook just got back from a month-long trip to India." She touched his arm lightly. "I have a lot of guy friends around town. None of which I'd like to kiss again." She turned and quickly darted out into the rain.

Well, shit, he thought as he locked up and headed upstairs. He had felt tired enough to fall into bed, but now he was full of energy as he thought about the possibility of kissing Avery again. So instead of showering and falling face first into bed, he spent the next two hours working on his apartment.

By the time he was done, the entire upstairs was clean enough to have guests. Sure, the floors up there could use sanding and a fresh coat of stain, but at least he had a massive area rug to cover most of the really bad boards.

He still didn't have much furniture, but he figured that he could head to his storage unit first thing in the morning and grab a few things. After all, he had to run back to Edgeview to get everything that he'd need to make Hannah and Wyatt's trial wedding dinner.

When he woke, it was to the sound of thunder. He groaned when he realized he'd slept through his alarm. Pulling himself out of bed, he dressed quickly and gathered everything he'd need to get his supplies for the day.

Since it was raining, and he didn't have a cover for his truck, he'd have to put off getting too many of his things out of storage.

The short drive on the highway to Edgeview was easy enough, as it was still too early for most people to be out on the weekend.

However, the quaint streets of Edgeview bustled with life as he navigated his truck through the familiar roads. He pulled up to the grocery store closest to his mother's place, the one store he knew for sure that he could find all the ingredients he needed for his special dinner.

As he stepped out of his truck, a knot tightened in his stomach as an old memory flickered in his mind. He hadn't thought about it in years. He and his parents had come here one rainy day to get groceries. His mother had been very pregnant with Sophia. He remembered that detail since she was moving so slowly with her very large belly, which had stuck out of the bright yellow raincoat she had on. He could still remember the sound of her rain boots, which had squeaked on the floor as they traveled down every aisle.

His father had been drunk. He didn't have to think hard to remember that fact since it was a rarity for his father to be sober.

About halfway through the family's outing, his father had gotten irritated at something and started pulling his mother down each aisle, as if to make her walk faster.

When his mother slipped and fell, he grew even angrier. The only thing that had stopped his father from kicking his mother as she lay sprawled out on the wet tile floor was the store manager rushing over to help his mother up.

That was one of the days that Lucas could remember understanding what his father was. What kind of monster had lived within the man?

Shaking the bad memories from his head, he dashed into the store.

As he moved through the aisles, picking up fresh vegetables, spices, and other essentials for his planned items, he tried not to think of all the times he'd been in this store with his father.

Edgeview was a town filled with memories, but none seemed to haunt him quite like the ones in this store did. It wasn't often that Lucas dwelled on his childhood, but here, amidst the fluorescent lights and neatly stocked shelves, the memories came flooding back with an intensity he hadn't anticipated.

Maybe his mind was returning to the past and his child-hood after hearing so many wonderful stories from Avery about her life. The difference between their childhoods was stark.

Forty minutes passed in a blur as he carefully selected each ingredient, his focus unwavering despite the unsettled feeling in the pit of his stomach. Just as he reached for the last item on his list, a voice sliced through the air like a knife, sending a shiver down his spine.

Diego.

Jerking his head around, he saw his father standing at the end of the aisle. The years had been unkind to him. The once-vibrant man was now worn down by time and the demons that obviously haunted him.

Lucas felt his entire body tense as his father's gaze locked onto his. Suddenly, a wave of apprehension washed over him like a tidal wave. He had hoped to never cross paths with the man who had brought so much pain into their lives, yet here he was, standing before him once again.

The smell of alcohol lingered in the air as Diego approached, his footsteps heavy with the weight of years of regret and resentment. Lucas's jaw clenched as he struggled to maintain his composure, his fists tightening around the handle of the grocery cart.

"What are you doing here, Diego?" Lucas's voice was low, barely audible above the hum of the store lights.

Diego's smirk widened, a glimmer of mischief dancing in his eyes, which unfortunately matched Lucas's so perfectly. Diego leaned in closer, invading Lucas's personal space with an air of entitlement.

"Heard you're opening up your place in Pride. Figured I'd come to congratulate you," he slurred, his words dripping with sarcasm. "Figured it was about damn time you paid me back."

"For?" Lucas's eyes narrowed.

"You owe me, boy, for what you done to me. The lies you told. All those years I lost." His father's words slurred even more.

Lucas felt his temper flare at the mention of his father's past sins, his resolve hardening like steel as he met the older man's gaze with unwavering determination.

"I don't owe you a thing," he spat, his voice barely containing his rage. "Not after what you did."

Diego's laughter cut through the air like a knife, drawing the attention of nearby shoppers who glanced over with curiosity and concern.

"You always were ungrateful, boy," Diego sneered, his laughter morphing into a cold, bitter edge. "It's about time you gave your father some goddamn respect."

Lucas felt a surge of anger boil within him, but he forced himself to stay calm, refusing to give his father the satisfaction of seeing him lose control.

"You lost any right to my respect that day, ten years ago," he growled, his voice barely above a whisper. "Now listen to me and listen well. You stay away from me, from Mom, from Sophia. You're not welcome here."

For a moment, a flicker of uncertainty crossed Diego's

face as he looked at Lucas's unwavering gaze. Hopefully, the weight of his words sank in like an anchor dragging him down into the depths of his guilt and shame from his past. Lucas doubted it, but at least the old man paused. Then, the moment was over.

"You can't tell me what to do, boy," he muttered, his bravado faltering slightly as Lucas took a step forward.

"Try me," Lucas whispered, his eyes blazing with anger and intensity. "If you even think about coming near my family again, you'll regret it."

With a final, defiant jerk of his cart, Lucas broke free from his father's hold and made his way to the checkout, his heart still racing from the encounter.

As he loaded his groceries into his truck and drove back to Pride, a sense of determination settled over him like a cloak. No matter what demons may resurface, he vowed to protect his family at all costs, just as he had all those years ago.

Chapter Nine

Avery, being Avery, arrived at Sunset Venue an hour earlier than Lucas had asked her to be there. She wanted time to chat with Kara and Robin and try to get a few more details about their cousin, if she could without raising suspicion.

To her surprise, however, Lucas was already there working in the kitchens. From the looks of it, he'd been there a while, too.

"Hey," she said, setting her bag down on the counter. "I thought you said to be here at three?"

He smiled at her. "I did. I've been here a few hours prepping a couple of the dishes." He motioned towards a massive slow cooker. "That one takes six hours to cook."

"Six..." She shook her head. "I could have come earlier."

He chuckled. "And done what? Watched the slow cooker with me?"

She shrugged and leaned on the counter. She wanted to tell him yes, but instead asked, "What can I do now?"

He glanced around. "Nothing yet. We're still a little early to do much."

"How about I make us some iced coffee?" she suggested after a moment.

His eyebrows shot up. "Can you?"

She laughed and then went to work making one of her favorite summertime drinks. It wasn't the first time she'd worked in the massive kitchens, nor, she doubted, would it be the last.

After making her special iced coffee drink for her and Lucas, he put her to work bringing in a few more groceries that he'd left in his truck.

An hour later, the clatter of pots and pans filled the spacious kitchen as Lucas and Avery worked side by side. They moved around the stainless-steel countertops, avoiding bumping into one another as if their movements were synchronized.

"All right, let's see what we've got here." He leaned over her shoulder and checked her work. He'd put her to the task of cleaning and prepping all of the vegetables by slicing off their stems and removing all of the seeds.

"How am I doing, chef?" she joked.

Lucas nodded approvingly, a smile tugging at the corners of his lips as he surveyed her work.

"Perfect." He glanced at his watch. "Looks like it's time to get started on the main course."

With a flick of his wrist, Lucas grabbed a cutting board and began to chop onions with precision. She was in awe of his knife skills, no doubt honed from years of working in the kitchen.

He gave her a new task of slicing the peppers and tomatoes, which she did with a lot less finesse than he had. Next to him, she was a flurry of quick and sloppy motions while still moving slow enough that she didn't slice off any digits. She had warned him that she wasn't as fast as he was but he'd just shrugged and told her that it didn't matter since everything she was chopping would eventually go into the blender to make sauces.

As they worked side by side, a comfortable silence settled over them, broken only by the rhythmic sound of chopping and the occasional sizzle of food hitting the hot skillet. She could tell that Lucas was in his element, lost in the simple pleasure of preparing a meal.

"You know, I think we make a pretty good team." She nudged his elbow as she stood close to him while he stood back to take a sip of his drink.

Lucas grinned and a warmth spread through her at the sight of his smile.

"Yeah, we do, don't we? Who knew my new business manager would also be my best sous chef?" he joked.

Avery chuckled as her cheeks grew heated at the compliment and the way his eyes were somehow penetrating deep into her mind.

"Well, what can I say? I'm a woman of many talents." She tried to brush off the embarrassment of blushing by turning away. Damn. She never blushed.

By the time the aroma of sizzling spices filled the air, she was lost in watching him work instead of helping out. Honestly, she felt more in the way than anything.

"So, any progress on picking a name for your restaurant?" she asked when he paused to take a sip of the water that she offered him.

Lucas flashed her a grin, his eyes sparkling with amusement as he flipped a tortilla in the pan.

"Oh, you know, I've been thinking about a few. How about Sabor de Lucas?"

Avery chuckled, her eyes gleaming with mischief as she answered. "Not bad, but what about Lucas's Cantina?"

Lucas laughed, shaking his head in mock disbelief.

"That sounds like a place where I'd serenade customers with my terrible guitar playing."

"You didn't gain any musical talent from your grandfather?" she asked, leaning on the counter.

"Nope. Not that he didn't try to teach me." He rolled his eyes. "After which he quickly told me to stick with cooking."

She laughed. Their banter was interrupted when his cousin Robin strolled into the kitchen. The woman looked even more uncomfortable today than she had on the beach.

"When are you due again?" she asked her.

"Not soon enough." She laughed. "Hopefully, I'll pop before your brother and Hannah's wedding."

Avery had liked Robin and her sister, Kara, instantly when they moved to town. Robin's warm smile easily lit up any room that she was in.

"How's it going in here?" Robin asked, leaning on the countertop next to her cousin's shoulder to look into a pan. "That smells amazing."

"Dinner will be ready right on time." He nudged her with his shoulder playfully then handed her an empanada that had been cooling on a dish.

Robin took it happily and nibbled on it as her gaze swept over the array of dishes already laid out on the countertops under the warmers.

"This all looks so amazing. You two make a great team." She motioned with an empanada between Avery and Lucas.

"That's why I hired her," Lucas joked. "I can spot a keeper." He winked at Avery over his shoulder.

Just then Wyatt and Hannah stepped into the kitchen arm in arm, laughing at something together.

Her brother looked giddy to have Hannah beside him.

Avery was thankful that he'd stopped being such an idiot and had finally come home to the one woman who had always loved him. The only one she had ever wanted to call her sister. Hannah was not only her best friend but her soul sister. Even if her brother hadn't gotten his butt in gear last year, Avery would have always thought of Hannah that way.

Seeing the couple's eyes light up at the sight and smell of the feast before them, a burst of pride rushed through her for Lucas.

"Wow, Lucas, this looks amazing," Wyatt said moving forward.

"Nope," Robin moved forward, blocking them. "You two are out here until everything is ready."

"I can't believe you're cooking all of this for us tonight just for a dry run," Hannah called over her shoulder as Robin nudged them back out the doors, no doubt to one of the tables she had set up for them in the large barn.

Sunset Weddings, or Sunset Venue as it was now called, had opened a while back after Robin and Kara moved into town. They'd purchased the massive barn structure along with a small cottage that sat just down a pathway. The first thing they'd done was turn the barn into a wedding and event venue. The remodeled barn was a marvel and one of the most romantic spots on the West Coast.

In the past years, there had been more weddings and parties in this old, renovated barn than there had been in the past fifty years in Pride put together.

People came from out of the country to get married there.

"It's the least I could do for the happy couple who might officially hire me to cater their wedding," Lucas said under his breath when they were alone again. "If I don't burn anything that is."

Avery chuckled. "Trust me. You've got this."

When Lucas added the final touches to each dish, what was laid out before them was nothing short of a culinary masterpiece.

Avery helped Lucas carefully cover each brightly colored dish with a warming lid. Then they loaded them onto several large trays. It took them each two trips to carry everything out to her brother and Hannah, who were sitting at a small round table in the center of the massive barn.

Avery knew that the space would be transformed into a magical setting for Hannah and Wyatt's wedding dinner. She'd witnessed the alterations to the barn for many events. For weddings or wedding receptions, dim soft-white string lights would hang from the rafters, giving the entire space a romantic atmosphere. There would be large round tables covered in soft-colored tablecloths with unique floral center-pieces. Flowers would adorn every corner, flooding the barn with sweet scents.

For birthday parties, the white lights would be replaced with colored ones. White tablecloths would be changed out for whatever color the birthday party planner requested. Balloons and streamers would hang from above or float freely everywhere.

The changes that Robin and Kara made to the place were nothing short of magnificent.

Tonight, the small round table was adorned with flickering candles and delicate flowers, a preview of the romantic atmosphere that would envelop the space on their big day.

The air in the barn was practically alive with anticipation as Lucas uncovered each plate. Wyatt's and Hannah's eyes lit up with excitement and their smiles widened each time a new dish was presented.

She stood by while Lucas sat each of the plates down with care and filled them in on the details of each dish.

She watched closely while Hannah and Wyatt took their first bites. Seconds ticked by in the quiet room until finally a chorus of appreciative murmurs filled the air. Only then did she and Lucas relax.

"This is incredible, Lucas. You've outdone yourself," Wyatt said between bites.

Hannah nodded in agreement and then pointed with her fork. "I want it all," she said with a chuckle. "It's all so very good."

Avery felt Lucas take a deep breath so she reached out and touched his arm.

"What is in this again?" Hannah asked as she took another bite of the food. "It's amazing," she said after Lucas answered. "Thank you both so much for doing this for us. It means the world to us." Hannah reached over and touched Wyatt's hand. "We wanted something special, something new and unique. How many weddings have we been to in the past few years? Not one has had this." She waved her hand over the table. "Nothing close to it. Not that the food wasn't good, but this, this is..."

"A-freaking-mazing," Wyatt said with his mouth full.

Everyone laughed as Hannah nudged him in the arm.

"Please, sit, join us. There's plenty," Hannah offered.

Avery felt her stomach growl. She motioned to Lucas and they moved two more chairs around the table.

"This place is the perfect spot for a wedding," Hannah said with a sigh, motioning towards the open barn doors.

Everyone looked in that direction. The Pacific Ocean

bathed in the warm hues of the setting sun, sat directly across the beach. It was a breathtaking view.

As Avery sat in the vast room, knowing that soon it would be adorned with flowers and twinkling lights and filled with chaos and family, she couldn't help but marvel at the simple beauty surrounding her. The soft glow of candle-light danced across the faces of their loved ones, casting a warm and intimate ambiance over the large empty room.

What she envisioned for her brother's and best friend's wedding day was a scene straight out of her childhood fantasies.

Her mind wandered back to her youthful dreams, where she would walk down the aisle wearing her mother's delicate lace wedding gown. In those dreams, she was always surrounded by a sea of smiling faces. She'd always envisioned the big day to be in a grand cathedral, with the scent of fresh flowers filling the air. But now, as she glanced around the table at the faces of family, her dreams shifted slightly.

Just as she was getting lost in her thoughts, Lucas's gentle touch brought her back to the present moment. His hand found hers under the table, and she felt a rush of warmth spread through her veins at his touch. With a soft smile, he mouthed two simple words, "Thank you," and Avery felt her heart flutter in response.

At that moment, Avery couldn't help but wonder what the future held for her. Was he the one she had been waiting for all along? The thought sent a thrill of excitement coursing through her, mingled with a hint of apprehension. But as she looked into his eyes, filled with nothing but adoration, she knew that whatever the future held, she'd enjoy the ride.

Chapter Ten

It was official. Lucas had been hired to cater Wyatt and Hannah's wedding. The worry and excitement about getting the menu just right kept him up for two nights after their trial dinner. He'd spent that time writing lists, making plans, and changing plans so many times that his head spun.

He had their preferred dishes from the sample meal he'd prepared for them. The rest had been left in his very capable hands.

Maybe the smell of the newly finished floor downstairs played a part in keeping him up at night as well. Since he and Avery had put the last layer of sealer on it a day ago, all they could do was wait for it to dry.

He itched to move his new tables and chairs onto it but knew better. Avery had informed him that it would be best to wait at least a week before putting anything heavy on the shiny wood floor.

Then again, his sleepless nights could be because he hadn't been able to get the encounter with his father out of his head. The man had looked comfortable in the store as if he frequented it a lot. But that couldn't be right.

He hadn't seen his old man in ten years. Surely he would have heard that the man was roaming around town before then.

He'd wanted to call his mother and warn her that Diego was back, but he didn't want to worry her. Instead, he'd called his grandfather and informed him of the run-in.

Even though he'd known his grandfather his entire life, Lucas had never been able to read the man's reactions. However, when he informed him that Diego was back in Edgeview, his grandfather's reactions were clear.

One of the first things Lucas had learned from him was a few choice words of Spanish. Several of them flowed from his grandfather during that short conversation.

After hearing the older man's promise that he'd watch out for his mother and Sophia, Lucas relaxed a little. He trusted that his mother knew how to kick his dad to the curb now. She may not have back then, but so much had changed over the years. His mother had changed.

She'd had three other successful relationships after his father had bailed. Three that had ended not due to abuse. Currently, his mother was seeing a man named Graig. Lucas had met the man on several occasions and liked the guy. He was an EMT at the hospital and had two grown kids of his own who lived in Chicago and a teenage daughter who lived with him full-time and was close friends with Sophia. Which is actually how his mother and Graig met. The biggest plus about that relationship was that he treated Sophia like his own daughter, even though he wasn't technically living with his mother. Yet.

Lucas had hopes that his mother would one day find her happy-ever-after. After all, he was a firm believer that if you spent a lifetime searching for love, you deserved to find it. Eventually.

After dressing and heading downstairs, he walked into the restaurant to find Avery already behind the bar, engrossed in her laptop.

Today, they would be sanding and painting the bar and countertop. He'd picked a bright blue color for the base. The countertop was wood and still in fairly great condition.

He had hopes of having everything else finished by the end of the new week. At least all of the major issues.

Parker and his crew had only a few days left in the building and had even agreed to install electric outlets for hanging string lights outside on the patio.

"What do you think of these?" she asked, not even glancing over her shoulder towards him.

He moved closer and looked over her shoulder. There on the screen were what appeared to be several small black iron tables, each with matching chairs that were all piled up on top of one another.

"They'd be perfect for the patio area." She glanced up at him.

He winced at the price but then remembered that he would be getting paid for the wedding in under a month and could just stretch out his budget.

"Yeah, they would. Where are they?" He leaned closer to see more details.

"Ruby's Antiques. I worked at the shop one summer after graduation. I thought I wanted to be an antiquary." She smiled up at him. "An expert on antiquities."

He chuckled. "Are there any jobs around here that you haven't done?"

She tilted her head. "I've never been a stripper." He almost choked on air. "Then again, we don't have many strip clubs in Pride." She poked him in the chest. "Jesus, you should see your face right now." She laughed as she turned back to her computer screen. "There, I asked Ruby to hold these for us. We can drive up there later today if you want?" She shut her computer screen down. "Once we're done painting this beauty." She tapped the bar countertop.

Lucas couldn't help but chuckle at Avery quickly changing the subject.

Her humor was a great amusement to him, and he admired the way her eyes sparkled with mischief. "You never fail to surprise me," he said, his tone affectionate. "Sounds like a plan," he replied, already envisioning the patio area of their restaurant transformed with those elegant iron tables and chairs.

With a shared sense of purpose, they turned their attention to painting the bar area.

They spent a few moments sanding the surface and taping off the edges. Before they began, they painted a small area of the bar with the color and used a heat gun to see the outcome.

"It's so cheerful," she said, leaning back. "It's going to be amazing."

"You don't think it's too wild?"

She laughed. "Trust me, it's going to be perfect."

As they started, he realized that she had brought color and excitement into his life in ways he never imagined possible. Maybe that was why he enjoyed adding the splashes of color to his restaurant. They reminded him of her.

With each stroke of the brush, Lucas found himself lost in the rhythm of their shared task. The rich blue hue gradually enveloped the once dull surface, transforming it into a statement piece that would undoubtedly draw the eye of every patron who stepped foot into their restaurant.

While they worked together, sitting on the newly refurbished floor covered carefully with tarps, Avery hummed a soft tune under her breath.

Lucas couldn't help but steal glances at her, marveling at the way her hair caught the light, casting a golden halo around her. He felt a surge of pride knowing that they were building something together, something that would leave an impression on her small town.

He couldn't stop watching her graceful movements as she happily worked. He was having such a difficult time focusing on the job that a large blob of blue paint landed on his knee.

Avery's laugh warmed him. "You have more paint on you than the bar." She handed him a rag to clean himself up.

"You have a very sexy humming voice," he said, taking the rag from her hand, letting their fingers brush and hold a little longer than necessary.

Her smile brightened. "Maybe I'll sing for you during one of those karaoke nights I plan on having to get customers in on weeknights." She nudged his knee with her own.

His eyebrows shot up. "That's a great idea. I knew hiring you was an ingenious move."

Her laughter echoed in the room. "Honey, hiring me was the best thing that could have ever happened to you and this place." She frowned suddenly. "Which needs a name." She glanced over to the chalkboard, which was now full of names. It was hard to decide. "What name did you get the building and the business permits under?"

He shrugged. "My name. I plan to file a DBA when I

settle on one finally."

She rolled her eyes. "Just pick one. We can't have everyone in town just calling it Lucas's place."

"Why not? It has a nice ring to it," he said, cleaning up his work pants. They now had so many blue spots on them, that he figured he'd either have to call it a new style or trash them.

She set her brush down and glanced at their work. "I know someone talented enough to paint the restaurant's name in this." She motioned to their work. "It might add a little splash. You know once we settle on a name and a logo. It can match the sign we hang outside."

He nodded. "Not a bad idea." The blue was nice, but it was lacking something.

Half an hour later, with the last stroke of paint applied, they stepped back to admire their handiwork. The bar gleamed with a newfound vibrancy, reflecting the happy atmosphere he hoped would flow once the doors were open.

Avery turned towards Lucas, a slight smile on her lips. "Another job well done."

Lucas reached out to tuck a loose strand of hair behind her ear, his touch lingering as he gazed into her eyes. "We make a pretty good team," he said softly, wishing more than anything he could kiss her again.

She leaned into his touch, a soft sigh escaping her lips. "The best team," she corrected him with a playful wink.

At that moment, surrounded by the scent of fresh paint and the warmth of her closeness, Lucas wondered if they would remain this close after the doors were open and the restaurant was so busy they barely had time to talk.

He'd just have to enjoy as much alone time as he could with Avery until then.

"How about we clean up and go see those tables?" she

said, dusting off her hands.

"Great." He glanced down at his paint-spattered pants. "I'll just head upstairs and change."

She nodded. "I brought a change of clothes too." She motioned towards her bag. "We can grab lunch. There's a food truck along the way that I love."

"Sounds perfect," he said, his voice tinged with excitement.

Together, they began to clean up their painting supplies before heading off to change. Being with Avery felt like coming home, a feeling he never wanted to let go of.

Once the last brush was rinsed and the paint cans neatly stored away, he made his way upstairs to his apartment to change. He pulled on a fresh pair of pants along with different shoes.

When he emerged from his apartment, he found Avery waiting for him, her smile radiant as ever. She had changed into a casual outfit of worn jeans and a soft pink T-shirt with yellow flowers on it that clung to her curves. The color highlighted the rich redness of her hair, making him want to reach out and run his fingers through the strands for hours.

As they made their way towards the door, Avery linked her arm with his playfully.

"I'm so ready to buy some stuff." Her eyes sparkled with excitement. "I love shopping and spending other people's money."

Lucas chuckled. With Avery by his side, he felt that anything was possible.

Lucas helped Avery into his truck and climbed in behind the wheel. As they headed out of town, he was thankful the rain had cleared up and the heat of summer was once more allowing the townspeople to enjoy the outdoors.

The small town still wasn't busy in comparison to Edgeview, but there were more people on the street. Avery rolled down her window and called out a hello to each of them they passed.

"It's rude not to honk or wave in town," she joked as she rolled up the window again when he hit the main road out of town.

"I'll keep that in mind. Where's this food truck?"

"Oh, just up here about two miles. My friend Carrie Brogan runs an animal sanctuary. On Saturday she makes burgers and hot dogs to draw people in to adopt or foster animals."

"Smart." He followed her instructions until he turned off the main road leading to the highway.

Carrie's Sanctuary was much larger and more grandiose than he would have imagined. There was a massive barn surrounded by goats, pigs, small donkeys, and a few horses. Three buildings circled a larger one in the center, which housed a food truck. More than a half dozen people sat around on picnic tables, enjoying the food. Almost every single person was holding a dog on a leash while they ate.

When they parked and got out of the truck, the aroma of freshly grilled food from the nearby food truck wafted through the air, teasing his senses and igniting his appetite. Avery's eyes lit up with excitement as she led the way down a wide pathway toward the food truck near the main building.

"Oh, I forgot to mention." Avery stopped in front of him. "You don't pay for the food with money." Her smile grew. "It's free, just as long as you walk a dog that's stuck at the sanctuary."

He nodded. "I like dogs."

Avery laughed and took his hand. "Come on, we'll go

break a couple of them out for a while and enjoy a burger."

It took them a little while to pick out a couple of smaller dogs, one brown terrier mix named Chunky and a small yellow doodle mix named Dave. They were given leashes by one of Avery's friends who worked there and set off to walk the dogs.

After strolling with them for a while around the grassy yard to let them relieve themselves, they headed over to the food truck. The old truck was adorned with colorful banners and twinkling lights and stood out from the grassy fields that surrounded it. There were two main dishes on the menu: burgers or hot dogs with a side of your choice of potato chips.

"The burgers are good," she said as they approached. "What do you want?"

"I could go for a burger," he replied, his mouth watering at the thought of sinking his teeth into a juicy patty topped with all the fixings.

Avery nodded in agreement, her eyes alight with anticipation. "Burgers it is!"

They approached the window of the food truck, where a friendly-faced girl greeted them with a warm smile. After placing their order, they found a cozy spot at a nearby picnic table and let the dogs sniff the ground while the aroma of sizzling meat filled the air.

As they sat there, basking in the warmth of the afternoon sun and the promise of good food and even better company, Lucas knew that he was exactly where he was meant to be.

"I don't think anything could be as perfect as this moment," he said with a sigh.

Just then, Dave lifted his leg and proceeded to soak his shoe while Avery laughed.

Chapter Eleven

fter Lucas washed his feet and changed into a pair of work boots he had in his truck, they dropped the dogs back off in their kennels and headed out to Ruby's.

When Lucas pulled the truck to a stop in front of the store, Avery's heart fluttered with a mix of nostalgia and excitement. The weathered old barn, with its patches of faded red paint and sagging roof, held a special place in her heart. It was here, among the oddities and treasures, that she had spent countless hours working alongside Ruby one summer. Out of all the jobs she'd had, this one had molded her the most.

"This place hasn't changed a bit," Avery remarked, a fond smile playing on her lips as she took in the familiar sight.

Lucas unbuckled his seatbelt. "When did you work here?"

Avery's gaze lingered on the rustic charm of the building. "The summer after graduation. It was my favorite job."

Together, they stepped out of the truck and made their

way to the entrance. The wooden door creaked open with a familiar protest, revealing the treasure trove of forgotten relics and vintage delights within.

Inside, the air was thick with the scent of old wood and dusty items and the best smell—that of so many books. Sunlight filtered through the dust motes, casting a warm glow over the eclectic assortment of items that filled every corner of the space in the massive barn.

Ruby stood behind the counter, her silver hair pulled back into a neat bun. The woman's eyes widened with delight as she caught sight of Avery.

"Avery, dear," Ruby exclaimed, her voice tinged with delight. "I didn't think you'd make it before I closed up for the night."

Avery's smile widened as she stepped forward to embrace Ruby. "It's good to see you, Ruby," she said, her voice filled with warmth.

Lucas watched the reunion, then greeted the woman after Avery quickly introduced him.

"We're here for the black iron outdoor furniture," he said easily.

Ruby's smile widened. "Ah, yes. Follow me," she said, leading them through the maze of treasures towards the back of the shop.

As they walked, Avery couldn't help but feel hints of deep nostalgia wash over her. It felt like coming home after a long absence, surrounded by familiar sights, smells, and sounds. She hadn't been back here in almost two years. Why? Maybe because everything in the small cottage she lived in now belonged to Brook. When she'd moved in, she hadn't even needed a television set or a bed.

Hadn't she always dreamed of hunting through the odd

items here to find a treasure to decorate her very own home one day?

Finally, they reached the corner stacked with metal-work pieces, and Avery's eyes lit up with delight at the sight of the elegant black iron tables and chairs.

"They're just as beautiful as the picture," she breathed, running her hand over the smooth surface of one of the tables.

Lucas nodded in agreement. "Perfect for our patio."

She wondered if he realized what he'd said. That he'd slipped and called it ours, instead of mine or the restaurant's. What did that mean? Maybe she was reading too much into it. Either way, she knew instantly that the tables would be perfect.

After finalizing the purchase with Ruby, Lucas, and Avery carefully loaded the tables and chairs into the back of the truck. Lucas was an expert at stacking everything neatly so they had plenty of space.

"Let's have one more look through the place before Ruby closes up. We may spot something else we need," she suggested.

He nodded and she took his hand and practically dragged him through the store.

She was just about to give up when she spotted a deep red leather sofa sitting along a back wall.

"Ruby." She waited until the woman came over to her. "How much for red here?"

Ruby smiled and then laughed. "For you, honey, I'll give you twenty bucks to take her off my hands."

"I couldn't..." Avery started, but when Ruby's eyebrows rose slowly, she knew better than to argue. "Deal." She held out her hand and then when Ruby hugged her, she held onto the older woman for a while. "Thanks," she whispered just before the woman stepped back.

"Looks like you got a sofa for your office," Lucas said as he helped her carry it outside to the truck.

"It's perfect," she said as they tried to maneuver it outside without bumping into anything. It was small enough to fit in the space without eating up too much room. It was comfortable and light so she could easily move it around herself if needed.

As they drove away from Ruby's, Avery couldn't help but feel a sense of gratitude for the memories she had made in that old barn. "I'll always cherish my time there," she said, her voice laced with nostalgia.

Lucas reached over to squeeze her hand. "One of my favorite jobs was my first job working at that Chinese place," he said, his eyes reflecting the same sense of humor. "Why did you never go back to work there?"

She shrugged. "Ruby couldn't afford it. I tried to donate my time when I found out she was having financial difficulties. But she's too full of pride." She sighed. "Besides, I had to pay my rent."

As Lucas pulled into the parking lot, Avery's gaze drifted over the familiar facade of the building. Memories flooded back as she remembered her days working at the sandwich shop. The building had changed so much in the short time that Lucas had owned it.

The anticipation of setting up the new iron tables and chairs on the patio added an extra layer of excitement.

They parked the truck and quickly unloaded the sofa and hauled it into her new office.

"It's perfect," she said, dusting off her hands.

"She was made for the spot," Lucas agreed. "Now, how about we conquer the tables and chairs?"

They unloaded all of the chairs first so they could get to the tables. Then they hauled everything over to the patio area.

"The bigger table should go here," she said, nudging the heavy thing into place. "The smaller ones, which will seat just two people, should go along each wall." She pointed.

"Agreed." He nodded and they quickly moved each table into place.

"See, now this area flows. No chairs can block the aisleways. We can have planters along here." She motioned. "With summer flowers to give the patio a little more privacy."

He stood back and let her rattle on for a while about her vision for the space. Next, they arranged the chairs at each table. The black iron gleamed in the sunlight.

"This is perfect," she said with a sigh.

"You enjoy this, don't you?" he asked, standing next to her.

"Of course." She glanced up at him, then spun around quickly as she glanced around the town. What they were doing to this place was changing the town, making it so much better for all who lived there.

As she looked up and down the street, she could see that each business took pride in bettering everything around them as well.

Then she laughed and motioned down the street. "You wouldn't believe the shenanigans I got up to in high school." She chuckled, moving one of the chairs a little. "Like the time Hannah dared me to climb up on the roof of the old movie theater." She motioned to the building, whose lights had just flickered on.

Lucas laughed, his eyes alight with amusement. "I bet that was quite the sight."

"My dad had to come get me down from the roof with the fire truck's ladder." She laughed. "I was grounded for a month after that one. Still, the view from up there was spectacular.

Without a word, he took her hand and led her inside the building. After heading up the staircase that led up to his apartment, he turned to a different doorway and opened it. Inside was another set of stairs.

"They just finished up here last week," he told her as he opened the last door at the top of the stairs. "I came up here the other night to watch the sunset." He stood back and nudged the door open the entire way.

Gasping, she stepped out onto the freshly renovated and tarred flat roof of the building. There was a slight dip towards the back of the building so that rain could drain to the half dozen scuppers and into downspouts.

Her eyes didn't even scan the recent patches that had been done. Instead, they zeroed in on the view in front of them.

This building sat on the corner of a five-point crossroads. Directly in front of it was Main Street. To the far right, Second Street started at Main and led further back into town, heading away from the Pacific Ocean towards the police department and the fire station. Then Main Street turned into the road that led off towards Jordan's Shipping, All in Bloom, Sunset Events, and the Hidden Cove neighborhood. Beyond that sat the lighthouse and state park area.

Front Street was the only straight street in the five-point connection. It ran from Pride's docks straight past this building and traveled by the grade school, the high school, and the Coast Guard training facilities before meeting with the highway that headed either towards Portland or, in the opposite direction, Edgeview.

This unique position of the crossroads allowed for the top of this building to have an unhindered view of the Pacific Ocean beyond the tops of the other buildings in Pride and the treetops and rocky shoreline.

The sunset was causing perfect bright pink streaks to cross the cloudless dark blue sky. The sun was no bigger than half the size of a quarter in the distance as the entire sky changed with each second that passed.

"It's so beautiful here," she whispered, wrapping her arms around herself.

"Better than the theater's roof?" he asked, stopping beside her and leaning on the high wall at the edge of the building.

"Without a doubt." She glanced at him. "Thank you for sharing this with me."

"Thank you for helping me bring my restaurant, my vision, to life," he said, his voice laced with gratitude. "For taking a chance on me and this place," he added with a slight shrug.

Avery easily stepped closer and wrapped her arms around him. "I'm glad I could be a part of it," she said, meaning every word deep down into her core. "I can't imagine not being here right now." She lifted onto her toes to press a soft kiss to his lips.

"I take back what I said earlier," he said as he pulled back.

"Hm?" She glanced up into his eyes.

"This time right here. With you." He wrapped his arms around her. "I don't think anything could ever be as perfect as this moment."

Chapter Twelve

The following day, Avery had off work. Her parents were finally returning from their trip to Hawaii. For some reason he couldn't explain, he was worried about running into them in town. It wasn't as if a few kisses signaled that they were an official item, even though he deeply wished it did.

Avery had made her intentions clear, hadn't she? As much as they could, they would try to keep things professional. Since she was the one making the move each time, he figured that this was her idea of not getting too close. Right?

God, he was so confused.

Lucas shook his head, trying to clear his thoughts as he entered the dining room. Today was about business. Since the moment he'd received the new tables and chairs for the main dining area, he itched to get them set up on the newly renovated flooring.

As he hauled each table and chair out of the storeroom in the back, his mind swirled with unanswered questions. With each piece he moved, he released some of the pent-up frustration that had built over the past few days.

Lost in thought, he didn't notice Avery approaching until she was standing beside him, a soft smile playing on her lips. "Hey," she said, her voice breaking through his reverie.

Lucas's heart skipped a beat at the sight of her. "Hey," he replied, offering her a small smile in return. "I thought you had the day off?"

"I drove by as I was heading to the store to get a few things for dinner tonight with my parents and saw you working in here." She glanced around. "I wanted to be here to help arrange everything." Avery's gaze softened, and she reached out to touch his arm. "Are you okay?" she asked, her concern evident in her eyes. "You look tired. Or worried."

Lucas ran a hand through his hair and realized that he was past due for a haircut. "Just tired," he finally said.

Avery nodded understandingly, her fingers lingering on his arm. "Want some help?"

Lucas looked into her eyes, seeing the concern and kindness there. "Yeah," he said, already feeling enormous relief, thanks to her presence. "If you want to help, that is."

Avery smiled quickly and rolled up her sleeves. "Put me to work. I have a couple of hours before my parents are due home."

As they worked side by side, he was grateful for her company. She immediately broke him out of his deeper thoughts with her cheerful conversation. She made him laugh more than any other woman he'd been interested in before.

When they finished arranging all of the tables and booths, the dining area looked inviting and welcoming, and his bad mood was completely forgotten.

After Avery left, he decided to head into Edgeview to meet his sister and mother for dinner. He'd sent them a text and told them he'd meet them at Sophia's favorite restaurant.

Stepping into the Italian restaurant in Edgeview, he waved to his mother and sister and made his way to the booth near the front window.

He instantly compared the soft warm ambiance of the Italian place to the happy, cheerful one he was creating.

He kissed his mother's cheek and sat next to Sophia. He flung his arm around his little sister's shoulders.

"This is nice," his mother said, shifting a little. "I'm glad you called. How is the place coming along?"

"I'll be ready to open the doors in a few weeks, maybe sooner. There's still a lot to do, plus I'm waiting for some of my kitchen equipment to get here. Oh, and I have to hire a staff." He laughed.

His mother chuckled. "I'm so very proud of you."

He glanced at his sister. "What's up, squirt?" He pulled his arm tighter around Sophia's shoulders for a makeshift hug.

"You'll never guess what happened to me today..." Sophia started. His sister's conversations always started the same way.

While she chatted animatedly about her day at school, her words punctuated by bursts of laughter, he hung on every word. Somewhere in the middle of his sister's story, they had all ordered their drinks and food.

Their mother watched as they chatted about Sophia's school drama with a slight smile on her lips. She looked happier than she had in years.

He wondered if it was due to Graig but didn't want to ask how that relationship was faring.

"You two always know how to brighten my day," she said, her voice filled with affection.

"Everything okay?" he asked her.

She sighed and then added. "I broke things off with Graig."

"Why?" he asked, concerned.

His mother shrugged. "I just don't think I can be my best self with him. I'm not sure I'm meant for happiness."

"Mom." He reached across the table and took her hand. "Everyone deserves happiness."

She nodded in agreement and just as Lucas reached for his drink, a voice cut through the air like a knife, freezing him in place. "Well, well, well. Look what we have here."

Lucas's heart plummeted as he turned to see his father standing in the doorway, his presence casting a dark shadow over their table.

His mother gasped and flung her arm out, as if shielding herself from an invisible blow, knocking over one of the drinks on the table. Then her expression hardened with anger and disbelief. "What are you doing here?" she demanded, her voice trembling.

His father ignored her question, his gaze fixed on Lucas with a predatory gleam in his eyes. "Isn't this picture perfect? The whole family is here having dinner," he said, his voice dripping with venom.

"Who is that?" Sophia whispered behind Lucas.

Lucas instantly tried to shield his sister from the man's view.

"I thought I'd drop by and see how my dear family is doing," Diego sneered. His eyes moved past Lucas to land finally on Sophia. "To see my baby daughter," he added loudly.

Sophia gasped behind him, and Lucas clenched his jaw while his hands curled into fists beneath the table.

Sophia's voice was barely a whisper. "Dad?"

His father's lip curled into a sneer as he turned all of his attention towards Sophia, his gaze cold and calculating. "That's right, my little princess," he said, his tone soft yet still sounding mocking somehow. "You've grown up since I last saw you."

His statement and tone caused Lucas to jump out of the booth and head towards the man. He had a firm grip on Diego's coat and was about to haul him outside when a waiter stepped over towards them.

The man was easily double Lucas's size and full of impressive muscles covered with faded tattoos. The guy was roughly Lucas's age and had even more Latin blood in him than Lucas did. The way he stood, the guy looked more like a bouncer than a waiter.

"Whatever this is, you'll need to take it outside. This is a family restaurant," the man said, clearly.

"He's not part of our family." Lucas jerked towards Diego. "If you call the police, I'm sure they can haul him away. There's no doubt he has at least one warrant out..." He dropped off when his father jerked free of his hold.

"I'm in no rush." Diego smiled. "Nice to see you again, Emily." He said his mother's name like it was a curse word. Then his smile turned bigger. "Sophia, I'll see you around." His eyes dipped to his sister's shirt and back up. "You sure have grown up," he said just before Lucas punched the man square in the jaw.

His father's body jerked back a step, knocking over a tray full of empty glasses.

"You son of a..." his father said, but then the waiter shoved between them.

"We've called the police," the man warned.

Suddenly, his father laughed, a harsh sound that echoed through the restaurant like a death knell. "You think you can keep me away?" he scoffed, his eyes flashing with malice. "I'll always be a part of this family, whether you like it or not." With a final glare, his father turned on his heel and stormed out of the restaurant.

"Sorry," Lucas said to the waiter with a sigh.

The man shook his head. "Assault is no joke. When the police get here..."

Lucas lowered his voice and quickly relayed why he had hit his father. The man's face paled and his gaze turned to where Sophia and his mother were huddled together in the booth. His mother was crying as Sophia held onto her with confusion written all over her face.

He understood that his sister had no clue why they were upset at the sight of the man. Nor did he or his mother have any plans to tell her anytime soon.

The waiter sighed and nodded after a moment of silence. "I'll send the police away and bring you some fresh breadsticks."

"Thanks..." He touched the man's arm.

"Rico," the man offered and disappeared.

Lucas sat across from his mother and sister as they held onto one another.

Silence descended over the table, broken only by the soft sobs and ragged breaths of their mother.

"Was that our dad?" Sophia asked when their mother grew quiet.

"Yes," his mother answered quickly. "I'm not crying because I miss the man. I'm crying because..."

"She hates him," Lucas finished. "We both hoped to never see that man again."

"Why?" Sophia asked, but then the table grew quiet when Rico delivered a fresh basket of breadsticks.

"Thanks," they all said to Rico.

"I've told the police about your dad. Told him what kind of car he was driving. Hopefully, they're out looking for him." His eyes moved to Sophia and his mother. "Can I get you anything else?"

"No, thank you." They both said together.

Rico smiled and nodded. "Your food will be out shortly."

"Why?" Sophia asked when they were alone again.

"I can't do this tonight," their mother said as more tears started. "We should just go home."

"No," Sophia said. "I'm sixteen. Old enough to know a little something about him."

Lucas sighed. "Diego was very abusive. When I finally could, I convinced him that it would be better if he weren't around."

"You're the reason he left?" Sophia asked him.

Lucas's chin rose slightly, and then he nodded. "I am."

Sophia seemed to relax a little. "I have one memory of that man. I couldn't remember his face until just now." Her eyes turned away from their mother to him. "Thank you for making him go away," his sister said, surprising him.

Lucas felt a knot in his throat and nodded as he reached for his drink.

"Now, let me finish my story," Sophia said with a grin before she picked up where she had left off in her earlier story.

By the time their food arrived, the three of them were laughing and had put the horrible ordeal behind them.

After paying for dinner, Lucas walked his mother and sister out to their car but instead of climbing into his truck, he headed back inside to find Rico.

"You, by chance, aren't looking for a different job are you?" he asked the man.

Rico frowned at him. "What?"

"I'm opening a restaurant in Pride and—"

"The new Mexican place?" Rico interrupted. "I've heard about it." He smiled. "We've all been eager for you to open your doors. I was keeping an eye out for the help wanted sign to go up."

Lucas chuckled and held out his hand. "I'll start interviewing in about a week. Swing by anytime."

"Thanks," Rico shook his hand. "It's a lot closer to home than this place. Besides, I don't know if you can tell, but I'm not Italian." Rico and Lucas laughed.

Chapter Thirteen

There were so many applications for Avery to go over the week after they put up the help wanted sign in the window. She'd printed the applications and had stuck them on the bar top for people to grab when they came inside.

Two days later, Avery sat behind her cluttered desk in her small office, a stack of resumes spread out before her. The soft hum of Parker and his crew finishing work somewhere on the outside of the building drifted in through the open doors.

She glanced over the first resume, her brow furrowing in concentration as she read the applicant's qualifications. After a few moments, she nodded to herself and set the resume aside in the stack of people she would schedule interviews with.

As she worked her way through the resumes, Avery found herself impressed by the diverse range of experience and skills displayed by the applicants. Who knew it was going to be such a hard job narrowing them down to the dozen or so crew members that they needed? Each resume told a unique story, a testament to the rich tapestry of backgrounds and talents that made up their small-town community. Of course, she knew almost every local applicant but was surprised at how many out-of-town people were in the mix. More than a dozen applicants were from Edgeview. Two of them were from Portland.

Just as she was about to move on to the next resume, there was a soft knock on the door, and a large Hispanic man stepped into the room, a nervous smile playing on his lips.

"Hey, Avery," he said, his voice tinged with excitement. "I'm Rico. Lucas told me to come on back. I'm looking to be hired on as waitstaff."

Avery's eyes lit up with recognition. Lucas had filled her in on running into the man the other night during dinner. The only thing he'd mentioned was that he was impressed with the man's skills and that she should hire him if she agreed.

"Of course, Rico," she said, motioning for him to take a seat on her new red leather sofa. "I'm glad you stopped by. Let's chat."

The man sat down, almost filling the entire sofa with his muscular form.

For the next half hour, Avery and Rico talked about his previous experience, his passion for food and hospitality, and his vision for the future. Rico spoke with enthusiasm and confidence, his love for the restaurant industry evident in every word. He spoke of his love for his family's heritage and the food that he desperately loved more than the Italian he'd been serving over the past year.

As the interview drew to a close, Avery couldn't help but be impressed by Rico's professionalism and genuine enthusiasm. With a smile, she extended her hand across the desk.

"Welcome to the team, Rico," she said, her voice filled with warmth. "I think you'll be a great addition."

Rico's face broke into a wide grin as he shook Avery's hand, gratitude shining in his eyes. "Thank you, Avery," he said, his voice filled with sincerity. "I can't wait to get started." He shifted. "I hate to ask, but what exactly is the name of this place?"

Avery laughed. "For now, we're calling it To Be Determined."

Rico laughed and nodded. "I wanted to chat with Lucas while I was here." He glanced out the door. "Is he around?"

"He's in the kitchen. They just delivered some of the equipment. Head on back if you want." He turned to go but she stopped him. "You wouldn't know of a good sous chef or bartender who is available, would you?"

Rico smiled. "I'll have Yolanda give you a call or stop by later this week. She's my on-again, off-again girlfriend."

Avery's eyes shot up. "You're okay to work together?"

Rico laughed. "Yeah, she's the mother of my unborn children but doesn't know it yet." He winked at her. "I'm just not smooth enough to ask her to marry me yet. The number one reason she keeps breaking things off with me." He chuckled. "Maybe this place, a new start, will give me the chance to finally take that leap. Adiós." He nodded and left.

After that, sitting in her office alone, she couldn't help but feel a sense of excitement for the future. With Rico and the other new hires on board, she knew that this place was poised for success, ready to welcome guests with open arms and delicious food for years to come.

Now all they needed was a name for the place.

An hour before quitting time, she had interviewed ten more staff, hiring six of them on the spot.

As Avery sat at her desk, reviewing the final stack of resumes, the door to her office creaked open, and the sound of familiar voices filled the room. She looked up to see her parents stepping inside, their faces glowing with excitement.

"There you are, Avery," her mother exclaimed as Avery jumped up from behind her desk and moved around to give her mother a warm hug. "This place has come a long way," her mother whispered.

Her dad followed her mother and stepped into her office with a warm smile, his eyes sparkling with pride. "You've done an amazing job with this place," he said, his voice filled with admiration. "You finally have your own office space." He nodded to the pictures she'd hung on the walls of her family. "Well done."

"Thanks, Dad," she said, her voice tinged with gratitude. "I'm finally able to do something I love."

Her mother glanced around the office, her eyes lighting up with curiosity. "This place is beautiful, Avery," she said, her voice filled with wonder. "You've made it your own space." She motioned to the red leather sofa. "I like this."

"We got it at Ruby's." Avery smiled.

Just then, Lucas stepped into the room. A warm smile spread across his face when he caught sight of Avery's parents. "Hey, Avery," he said, his voice warm with greeting. "I see you've got some visitors."

Avery nodded, returning Lucas's smile with one of her own. "Mom, Dad, this is Lucas," she said, gesturing toward him. "The owner of the restaurant and my new boss."

Her father extended a hand toward Lucas, a friendly smile on his face. "Nice to meet you, Lucas. We like what you've done to the place so far. Thanks for giving our girl a chance."

Lucas shook her dad's hand firmly, his gaze meeting the older men with genuine respect. "It's my pleasure, sir," he said, his voice sincere. "Avery's been a huge asset to me. I'm not sure I'd be this far without her."

Amber blushed slightly and beamed at the exchange.

"We're so glad. She couldn't stop talking about everything you've done here. We just had to come see the place for ourselves," her mother added.

"How about a tour?" Lucas offered. "We just had the rest of the kitchen equipment delivered. Parker and his crew just finished hooking up the gas stoves about half an hour ago." He motioned towards the door.

"Sounds wonderful." She took her father's arm and followed Lucas out the office door.

As they made their way out of the office, her mother turned to Avery with a mischievous twinkle in her eye as she mouthed "He is cute" to her. But then she said. "We'll have to come back for dinner sometime," she said, her voice filled with excitement. "I can't wait to try out the food."

Avery held in a chuckle and said, "I'll make sure to save you a table," as she followed them out of her office.

Lucas chatted about everything they had done in the past few weeks as he led her parents through the quiet empty restaurant and made their way toward the kitchen. Avery followed close behind, her heart brimming with pride as she watched her parents explore the space that she and Lucas had worked so hard to create.

As they stepped into the kitchen, her parents' eyes widened with wonder at the sight of the gleaming stainless-steel appliances and neatly organized prep stations.

"This place is incredible," they both marveled.

"What a change from the sandwich shop," her mother said, touching her arm.

Avery's eyes ran over the new appliances and she couldn't agree more. Those spots had been empty earlier that morning, making the space seem undone. Now, everything was finally in place. This was a real kitchen. Ready for staff, ready for food. The restaurant was ready for customers. Almost.

Avery nodded in agreement, her gaze sweeping over the rows of pots and pans hanging from the walls.

"You've outdone yourself, Lucas," her mother said easily.

Lucas stepped forward, gesturing toward the line of gas stoves where Parker and his crew had just finished installing the new stoves. "This is where all the magic will happen," he said with pride. "We're still getting everything set up, but we're getting close. Your daughter has been busy hiring all of the staff to make this place run smoothly." Lucas's eyes landed on her and she smiled.

"Only a few more hires to go." She beamed. Lucas nodded in appreciation.

"It's clear that you've put a lot of thought and effort into this place," her dad broke in. "So what are you going to call it?"

Avery chuckled as Lucas sighed and glanced at her. "I have a name picked out. But I'd like to keep it a surprise."

"You do?" she asked, curiously.

Lucas nodded. "Opening day, all will be revealed." He winked at her.

Her mother chuckled. "I see, you want to keep us all in the dark."

Lucas laughed. "I've got to guarantee this place will be packed on opening day somehow."

"Smart move." Her father slapped Lucas on the shoulder and then sobered up. "My guys will be by later this week for your fire inspection."

"Right." Lucas cleared his throat. "Parker has informed me he works hand in hand with your crew and swears we'll be ready."

Her father nodded. "He's good at his job. Just as long as you listen to him, we'll be okay."

Lucas held out his hand. "I'll keep out of his way as he hooks up the appliances just as long as he doesn't tell me how to cook."

Her father laughed as he shook Lucas's hand. "We'll get along great."

As they continued the tour, Avery watched her parents' reaction to Lucas closely. It was obvious to her that the three of them were getting along great. With her parents by her side and Lucas leading the way, she knew that she was exactly where she was meant to be.

Once they returned to the front of the restaurant, she and Lucas stood back and watched her parents leave hand in hand.

"I like them," Lucas said softly when they were alone again.

"They liked you." She turned to him.

"I was so nervous," he admitted with a puff of breath.

"They were too." She laughed. "My dad's hands were probably sweaty."

"I couldn't tell, because mine were sweaty too." He laughed.

"So, as the manager of this place, I think it's only fair that I get to know the name before opening day." She leaned closer to him.

Lucas laughed and shook his head and turned to walk

back towards the back of the place. "Nope. I like keeping some things secret."

She grabbed his arm and spun him around near the bar. "I'll bet I can get it from you," she teased, pinning him up against the bar.

"Oh? I don't know about that." Lucas's hands moved to her hips.

She moved closer and pressed her body up against his, pleased to see the heat of desire flash behind his dark eyes.

"Avery." His voice was a low rumble.

"Lucas," she whispered, her eyes moving to his lips. "Tell me," she said, inches from his lips as she watched his eyes close on a soft moan.

"You're killing me." His hands moved slowly over her hips.

She'd wanted to kiss him again. Every time she thought of it, she talked herself out of making the next move. After all, she was the one who had decided they should try and be professional. However, today, after her talk with Rico, the way the man talked about Yolanda, something had changed.

The longer she was around Lucas, the more she wanted him. Did he feel the same? She had to know. Needed to know.

"I've changed my mind," she said softly.

"About?" His hands fisted, balling material from her shirt inside them.

She smiled. "I don't think we can be just professional."

"No?" His eyes locked onto her lips.

"No." She shook her head. "Lucas?"

"Hm?" His eyes jerked up to hers.

"Take me upstairs," she whispered before pressing her lips over his.

Feeling the power behind his kiss assured her that he felt as much about her as she did about him. Seconds ticked by before he spun her around and lifted her into his arms.

Chapter Fourteen

Lucas didn't know what he had done in his life to deserve Avery. The moment he knew that she wanted him as much as he wanted her, he felt as if he was the luckiest man on the planet. Feeling her body melt against his, he was powerless to deny the attraction he had felt for her since the first moment he'd seen her in the silly elf outfit last Christmas.

The green tights she'd been wearing then were almost as sexy as the skin-tight black ones she had on now. He had been thankful he'd had a busy day to keep his mind from focusing on her curves.

When Avery whispered, "Take me upstairs," there was no way he could deny her. Thoughts of sweeping her up in his arms and carrying her up the stairs to his bed played in his head.

Then reality sunk in.

"My mattress is still on the ground," he groaned.

She shrugged. "Doesn't matter." She brushed her lips against his again. "Being with you is all that matters." Her eyes locked with his. "But if it bothers you, we could always go to my place." She smiled and added, "Next time."

He groaned with pleasure at the possibility of being able to have a second shot at this, even though there hadn't been a first-round yet.

Even if he couldn't give her candlelight and a real bed, he could show her just how he felt about her.

He lifted her and walked slowly towards the door that led upstairs. It took a lot of his concentration not to trip or, worse, drop her as he opened the door, climbed the stairs, and stopped just inside his bedroom.

"I like your place." She chuckled against his lips.

"Later, I'll give you a tour." He kicked his shoes off and took the kiss deeper than before.

The weeks of dancing around touching her had gotten to him. When her body slid down his and her feet touched the ground, his hands were finally free to roam over her.

Still kissing him, she pulled his shirt up and over his head. Then, when he was free of that barrier, she ran her hands over his tanned, toned chest and arms, down his body, and started pulling on his jeans.

"Easy," he sighed and took her hands in his. "We've got time. At least I hope so." He chuckled.

"I don't need time, Lucas." Her eyes met his. "I need you. Now." She pulled on his jeans as her smile grew. "We both knew this would happen sooner or later." He watched her suck her bottom lip between her teeth.

"I'm just thankful I wasn't the first one to cave," he said with a grin.

Her eyes narrowed. "You are very strong-willed."

His eyes slowly ran over her body. With the tips of his fingers, he traced the straps to the tank top she was wearing, nudging each strand off her creamy shoulders. "Not really.

I've been busy. If I hadn't, this would have happened a lot sooner," he assured her.

Her smile warmed him and when he stepped closer and covered her mouth with his again, he knew that even if he had a hundred years to show her how much he wanted her, it would go far too fast. He hoped to take a lifetime exploring her.

As their kiss deepened, Lucas felt a rush of desire coursing through his entire body. She had set off a fire that had been smoldering between them since that first flirtatious encounter. With each touch, each caress, he felt himself falling deeper under her spell, lost in the intoxicating allure of her presence, her smell, her taste.

With practiced ease, his hands moved with purpose, eager to shed the layers between them and revel in the raw passion that simmered just beneath the surface. Until they were both skin against skin. Heat against heat.

As he felt her fingers trace the contours of his skin, a shiver of anticipation ran down his spine, sending sparks of electricity along his nerves. His mind had shut off while his needs controlled him. Now, however, when they knelt on his bed, his brain called out to him to at least take care of one important task.

Reaching over, he grabbed one of the condoms he'd put on his makeshift nightstand the other day.

Avery smiled as he returned to her. "See, you at least have some of the bases covered."

He chuckled. "Tomorrow, I'm heading to Edgeview and hauling the rest of my furniture over here."

She nodded and then pulled him back down to her and kissed him until he was once more lost in the passion.

Their movements were frenzied yet tender, fueled by a hunger. As their bodies pressed together, the world around him faded into oblivion, leaving only the two of them entwined in a dance of desire and longing.

When she wrapped her hand around his length, he grasped her gently and they moved together until he was on the cusp of losing control.

Nudging her down until she lay on the bed, he shifted to settle his shoulders between her thighs. The first taste of her had both of them crying out with delight.

He surrendered himself fully to the moment, his senses overwhelmed by the heady rush of pleasure that enveloped them both. When he felt and tasted her convulse against his mouth, he slid on the condom and covered her body with his own.

"Whatever happens now, there's no going back," he warned.

To his surprise, she laughed and dug her nails slightly into his shoulders. "Don't hold back on me," she said with a smile.

A while later, they lay in his bed listening to the light rain outside.

In Avery's arms, he found solace, redemption, and a love that transcended all boundaries. Lucas knew with absolute certainty that this was just the beginning of their journey together, a journey filled with endless possibilities and the promise of an adventure like he'd never had with anyone before.

Avery was different than what he would have imagined for himself. She was better than he could have even dreamed.

He heard her stomach growl, and his followed almost immediately.

Laughing, Avery shifted slightly. "We forgot to have dinner."

"Yeah, I guess we had our minds on other things." He frowned. "I think I even forgot to lock the doors downstairs."

"It's a good thing we're in Pride." She shifted to look down at him. Her long red hair fell all around her face and shoulders.

She looked like a pixie, a goddess, the woman he wanted to spend the rest of his life with in this very bed.

Reaching up, he cupped her face and pulled her down for a kiss. Her stomach growled again.

"Okay." He laughed with her. "Food first." He shifted and climbed out of bed. "We'll use the kitchen downstairs so we can lock up."

He pulled on his jeans, glancing over as she put on her yoga pants again and then, to his surprise, tugged on his T-shirt. She looked sexy as hell in his shirt, even with it hitting her mid-thigh.

"Look on the bright side. Now you can try out your new ovens." She took his hand and followed him downstairs.

"Right," he said, holding the door open for her.

As the rain continued falling outside the newly renovated kitchen, he settled on making them some scrambled eggs with ham and toast.

As he cracked eggs into a bowl and whisked them with practiced ease, Avery jumped up on the countertop to watch him work.

Lucas couldn't help but chuckle at the sight, the contrast between Avery's casual attire and the elegance of the newly renovated professional kitchen.

"I love watching a sexy man make me a fancy meal at an ungodly hour during a rainstorm."

Lucas rolled his eyes playfully. "It's just eggs," he

replied, his tone laced with amusement. "Nothing too fancy."

"Anything I don't have to make myself is a culinary masterpiece. Trust me." She laughed.

"Well, it's not much," he added, feeling a little self-conscious and wondering if he should have done something better for them.

As he poured the eggs into a sizzling skillet, Avery hopped off the countertop and sauntered over to him, her movements fluid and graceful.

"I'm sure they'll be delicious," she said, her voice filled with confidence. "After all, everything tastes better when it's made with passion." She leaned up and traced her mouth over his jaw.

When he reached for her, however, she stepped away. "I'll get us something to drink." She walked over to the large refrigerators.

"There's some orange juice," he called out as she disappeared inside. With a flick of his wrist, he expertly scrambled the eggs. The familiar sound of their sizzle somehow comforted him and had his racing heart rate slowing.

How many times in his youth had he turned to cooking to find inner peace? So many.

"You love this, don't you?" she asked, setting a glass of juice beside him.

He smiled and nodded. "It's my passion."

Her eyes dulled a little as she looked down. "I didn't know what my passion was"—her eyes moved up to his—"until recently. This place, it's filled something inside me that no other job has."

He shifted and wrapped his arm around her as he turned off the flame. "You and me both." He kissed the top of her head.

As they savored their late-night meal, they talked about other passions they had and went over plans for opening day, and she filled him in on each of their new hires.

"So, what's your favorite thing to do on a lazy Sunday afternoon?" Avery asked with a yawn as they headed back upstairs.

Lucas sighed, a thoughtful expression crossing his face. "Besides cooking, I love taking long walks in the park," he replied, his voice tinged with nostalgia. "There's something about being surrounded by nature that just soothes the soul."

Avery nodded in agreement, a smile playing at the corners of her lips. "I couldn't agree more," she said. "There's nothing quite like the feeling of the sun on your skin and the sound of birds chirping in the distance. I love running. Early mornings are best."

"I've been known to run. Once I'm settled in a schedule that is."

"I haven't been in a few days. Maybe we can run together sometime?"

"I'd like that," he said.

As they settled back in bed, she asked, "What about movies? Do you have a favorite genre?"

He grinned, knowing that this was a topic he could talk about for hours, even though she had been yawning since halfway through the meal.

"I'm a sucker for action films," he admitted. "There's something exhilarating about watching the hero triumph against all odds."

"I'm more of a romantic comedy kind of girl," she replied with another yawn. "There's nothing like a good love story to lift your spirits and warm your heart."

He pulled her into his arms. "My television is in storage."

She chuckled. "We can watch a movie some other night. Right now, I'm far too tired."

Then she surprised him by rolling over on top of him, her legs caging him in. "At least for a movie." She leaned in to brush her lips across his.

Chapter Fifteen

As the soft rays of morning sunlight filtered through the curtains that hung over his living room windows, Lucas stood at the stove, humming a tune as he moved about the kitchen, the tantalizing aroma of sizzling bacon and freshly brewed coffee filling the air.

They had showered together, enjoying each other slowly, and she'd realized that it was the first time she'd ever showered with a man. Feeling too embarrassed to tell him that, she appreciated every single touch and moment she could.

It had taken her a while to comb through her hair and when she stepped into the kitchen, he'd handed her a cup of hot coffee.

She watched Lucas with interest as she sipped the coffee. He did a little twist while he flipped a piece of toast in the pan. "You're chipper this morning," she said, smiling.

"You aren't?" he threw back at her, and she laughed.

When he set a plate of bacon and French toast in front of her, she groaned with pleasure.

"Keep feeding me like this and I'll have to go on a diet," she warned.

Lucas brushed a stray lock of hair from her face, his touch so gentle. "You're perfect no matter what," he said simply, his gaze never leaving hers.

Together, they sat down to enjoy their meal, the simple act of sharing breakfast filling them with a sense of warmth and contentment. As they laughed and talked, Avery couldn't help but feel grateful for the man sitting across from her. He'd given her more purpose in the short time they'd known one another than anyone else ever had.

He'd trusted her with far more than just a job. This was his baby. His passion. It was so obvious to anyone who had ever watched him cook.

Each day she worked here, her passion for the place grew. She needed to see this through. No matter what.

After breakfast, they cleaned up the kitchen and did the dishes together. With a satisfied sigh, Lucas turned to Avery. "Care to head to Edgeview with me?" he asked, his voice tinged with anticipation.

"Absolutely," she replied.

The moment they stepped out of the building and into the bright sunshine of the morning, she felt a swell of happiness hit her. This was where she wanted to be. The day was going to be perfect.

Hand in hand, they walked towards his truck, greeting every person they saw along the way.

"I guess the news will be out about you staying with me last night," he said once they were in his truck.

"Oh, I'm sure everyone knew last night," she joked. "It's hard to keep secrets in a small town. Is that a problem?"

"No," he answered quickly and took her hand in his. "For you?"

She shook her head. "No. If it were, I would have insisted we head to my place. It's a little more off the pathway than leaving my car parked overnight in a lot at one of the main intersections in town."

"Right." He nodded and started heading out of town.

"How much stuff do you have?" she asked as he drove.

"Not much. I was hoping to buy some of the necessities after I opened and sold a lot of my older stuff. I have a newer sofa and chair, coffee table, bed frame, and nightstands, and that's about it. A bunch of boxes of things my mother saved of mine over the years." He chuckled. "Drawings I did when I was a kid that should have been tossed years ago."

"My mother has two boxes of my stuff in her attic. I swore to her that if she tried to give me any of it, I'd have a bonfire that night."

He laughed as he drove towards Edgeview. They continued to talk about their childhoods while the scenery whizzed past, a blur of green fields and winding country roads. Avery leaned back in her seat as Lucas told her the story about the day after his sister was brought home.

The stories reminded her of the pictures she had of the day her parents had brought Wyatt home. Even though she was too young to remember, it was the only proof that she was indeed older than her brother. Because she was a lot smaller than him, Wyatt always joked when they were younger that his parents had gotten confused and that he was actually older than her.

Lucas glanced over at her. "I'm glad you're coming with me," he said, taking her hand in his. "It means a lot to have you by my side."

Avery returned his smile, her heart fluttering at his

words. "I wouldn't miss it for the world," she replied, her voice filled with sincerity.

The rest of the drive passed in comfortable silence. As they pulled into the parking lot of Lucas's storage unit, Avery couldn't help but feel a pang of curiosity about his previous life in Edgeview and what he would have in his storage unit.

"This is my unit," he said, his voice tinged with pride. When he opened the metal door, she realized he hadn't been joking. Inside sat a brown leather sofa, a cream-colored headboard for his bed, a metal bedframe, two nightstands, a newer coffee table in soft light wood, and a few lamps and boxes.

To her surprise, a beautiful black Harley Davidson sat in the back of the unit.

"You have a bike?" She walked over to it and ran a finger over the flawless paint job.

"I do. When I have someplace to park it besides the street, I'll bring her to Pride." He smiled.

"She's a beauty." She didn't know much about motorcycles but loved riding on them. Her brother had one a few summers back and had taken her on many rides.

"We could take her for a spin," he suggested. "If you want."

"Yes," she said, sounding a little too eager.

"Okay, let's get everything cleared out first. We should be able to get it all in one trip." He stepped over to the furniture. "The sofa should probably go first, which means, we have to move everything else out to get to it." He glanced at her. "A quick warning, this sofa is a lot heavier than your red one."

She nodded. "I can handle it."

"We'll go slow." He handed her a lamp. "For now, let's

set everything over here." He took another one and set it off to the side.

Whenever she'd moved things with her family, Wyatt, and her dad did all the heavy lifting while she and her mother stood back.

But Lucas was counting on her to help him with the heavy sofa and, for the first time in her life, she was grateful she could help. The men in her family treated her like she was fragile and too weak. Lucas didn't.

They got the sofa and the rest of his things safely into the truck, including his massive flat-screen television, which he'd put in the back seat. She couldn't help but wonder how they were going to haul the sofa up the stairs to his apartment.

"Here," he said, handing her a helmet and then helping her put it on. She stood by while he pulled on his helmet and then rolled the bike out of the garage.

"Will your truck and things be okay here?" she asked.

He nodded. "Yeah, the place is gated. Hop on."

She lifted her leg over and slid behind him, wrapping her arms tightly around him.

"Ready?" he asked.

"Yes," she said, enjoying the feeling of him against her and the bike under her.

Once they were out of the storage unit, he slowly weaved through the back roads until they hit the open country road. They left the straight streets lined with homes with perfectly manicured yards and started passing fields filled with alfalfa, tall grasses, cattle, horses, and even goats. The smells of the small city were replaced with dirt roads, country air, and, to her mind, home.

She didn't have to wonder why anyone would love traveling like this. With the warm breeze on her face, she felt more alive than she had in years.

"How are you doing back there?" Lucas asked when they stopped at a stop sign.

"Wonderful." She sighed. "We should do this more often."

"Agreed. I've missed going out on her. Ready to head back?"

She groaned a little. "I suppose."

He chuckled. "Next day we have off, I'll take you on a longer ride."

"Deal."

He made a U-turn and headed back the way they'd come.

By the time he pulled into his storage garage, she was addicted to riding.

"I need to stop off at my mother's place quick and then maybe we can head to Baked for some pizza before unloading everything," he suggested.

"Sounds great." She sat back to enjoy the drive to his mother's house. The one-story ranch home wasn't far from the storage unit.

Lucas pulled into the driveway and parked next to a deep blue sedan. He turned off the truck and frowned.

"What?" she asked, suddenly concerned.

"My mom should be at work." He glanced at his watch. "She always works Sunday afternoons." He got out of the truck and she followed him up the sidewalk to the door.

"Mom?" Lucas called out after unlocking the front door. "Sophia?"

A banging sound came from somewhere in the home. Lucas took a step forward and then stilled when his mother called out.

"Back here. I'll be out." Her voice sounded strained.

She felt his tension double when his mother stepped out from the hallway towards their left. Her hair was slightly messed up, and she had a scared look on her face. It was obvious she had a black eye and was trying to hide it with her hair. She'd been crying and her shirt was ripped in a few places.

"Where's Sophia?" he asked, moving closer.

"She's at a friend's house," his mother answered loudly, glancing backward.

"Mom?" Lucas asked as a tear slipped down her cheek. He took her shoulders gently, and she cried out as if he'd broken her.

"He's got her," his mother whispered to Lucas against his chest.

Lucas shot through the house, rushing back to where his mother had just come from.

Avery was there to catch Lucas's mother, who fell into her arms, crying out in pain just before passing out.

After settling Emily on the floor, she pulled out her phone and dialed 911. She had seen the numbers on the door of the house and easily told the dispatcher the address as she heard the sounds of a fight happening in the back of the house.

When Sophia ran into the room, a wild look in her eyes, and spotted her mother on the floor, she rushed to her side. Sophia looked worse than her mother did. Her left cheek was red and swollen. Her lip was bleeding and her hair was in tangles. The girl's clothes were torn and messy like Emily's were.

"Mom!" Sophia cried. Then she looked up at Avery. "He's going to kill him. Help him," she pleaded.

Fear for Lucas shot through her so quickly that she

jumped up and rushed down the hallway to the sounds of the fight.

When she entered what appeared to be his mother's room, Lucas was on the floor hovering over a man and punching the guy over and over again.

"Lucas!" Avery shouted and rushed to stop his next blow. "He's unconscious," she said after seeing the man's eyes closed.

Lucas stilled the moment she touched his arm. "Son of a..." He dropped off as he stood up, standing over the man as if waiting for him to jump up again. "Sophia?"

"She's with your mother," Avery answered.

The room was a disaster. Avery didn't know if the fight had caused the damage or if something had happened before they'd arrived. Since the rest of the home was spotless, she could tell that the mess wasn't normal.

"Did you happen to call the police?" Lucas asked.

"Yes, they're on their way." She held onto his arm. "Is that..."

"Diego." He nodded, knowing that she was going to ask if the unconscious man on the ground was his and Sophia's father. He sighed. "Are they okay?" He motioned towards the door.

"I'll go check." She turned towards the door.

Both of them had their focus off the man on the floor for a split second. One minute Lucas was standing next to her and, the next, he was falling towards her as Diego pulled on his legs.

They hit the ground with a thud and, thanks to Lucas controlling the fall a little, she landed beside him instead of under his full weight.

Diego jumped up and sprinted past them, out of the door and down the hallway.

By the time they heard Sophia scream, Lucas was up and chasing after the man.

Avery followed, ignoring the ache in her ankle and elbow where she'd landed awkwardly seconds before.

Sophia was fighting the man as he tried to pull her towards the front door.

Lucas rushed towards them, screaming for Sophia to duck. His sister jerked her body to the side just as Lucas body-tackled Diego. The pair of them flew out the front door, crashing through the wood door and sending splinters flying all over Sophia, who had fallen just inside it.

Seeing Lucas and Diego disappear out the door was the scariest thing she'd ever witnessed. She'd seen moves like it in action movies, but never in real life, and especially not with a man she'd just spent the night with. A man she hoped to spend a lot more time with in her future.

Her screams echoed in the house as she rushed forward to see if she could help Lucas in any way.

She saw three armed men in black heading towards them and running up the sidewalk, and it took her a few seconds to register that they were the police.

They pulled Lucas off Diego as they screamed for everyone to get their hand up, and she froze in place.

Then she too was shoved from the side and pushed back into the house.

"I called," she cried out to the officer moving towards her. "He's my boyfriend. Diego is the one you want." She pointed to Lucas's father.

Her cries didn't stop the officers from securing both men in handcuffs, face down on the sidewalk and front yard.

Lucas went still, complying with the officer's demands

and talking in soft tones while Diego fought and kicked out, still trying to get away.

"That's my son," Emily shouted from the doorway. "He was protecting us from him." She pointed to Diego. "He broke in earlier this morning and held my daughter and me hostage until my son came."

Avery rushed over when the woman leaned heavily against the doorjamb. Carefully, she held onto her so she wouldn't fall again.

"Ma'am." An officer turned towards them. His eyes moved up and down Lucas's mother. "I'll call a female officer to come take your statement."

"My daughter is hurt," Emily said with a sigh. "We both are."

"Do you require an ambulance?" the officer asked while the other two officers hauled the still-fighting Diego up off the ground. Lucas was still handcuffed and lying still while they fought to control his father.

"Yes, please," Emily answered the man.

"I'm taking her inside to sit down until it comes," Avery said and then helped Lucas's mother inside. She caught Lucas's eyes as she did so and could see his worry disappear as he smiled at her and whispered, "Thanks."

Chapter Sixteen

It wasn't Lucas's first time being handcuffed by the police for a misunderstanding. However, it was the first time he was let go without being hauled down to the station and fingerprinted.

Thanks to his mother quickly telling the female officer what had happened, he was released to follow the ambulance carrying his sister and mother to the hospital.

He hadn't heard the entire story of what they had gone through in the preceding hours, but he'd heard enough.

Diego had barged in that morning when his mother was just about to leave for work and held the two of them hostage. Both his mother and Sophia had fought Diego as best as they could.

When they reached the hospital, his mother demanded they check Sophia first. The pair of them were wheeled in different directions.

"Go with her," his mother begged him, motioning towards Sophia.

"Stay with my mom?" he asked Avery, who nodded quickly as he rushed to follow Sophia.

"I'm okay," Sophia told him when he caught up with her as they were wheeling her into a small curtained area.

He took his sister's hand in his and noticed they were cracked and red as if she'd punched something or someone.

"Did he hurt you?" he asked softly. His sister didn't get a chance to answer, as he stepped aside for the nurse to check on her.

He stood in the corner as his sister explained where she hurt and her pain levels.

The nurse decided to send her for an X-ray of her wrist. She also thought she might have a concussion.

"Can I go with her?" he asked the nurse.

The woman smiled and nodded. "You're her..."

"Brother," he added quickly.

"Do you need someone to look at your lip and eye?" the nurse asked softly, moving closer to him, and reaching up to touch his cheek.

There had been a time when he would have returned her flirtations.

"No, thanks," he said with a nod. "My girlfriend will see to them later."

The nurse sighed and shrugged. "Let me know if that changes anytime soon." She winked and then turned back to his sister. "You're one lucky girl, having such a kind brother to look out for you."

"I know it," Sophia said and then, to his horror, she burst out crying.

He rushed to her side and held onto her while she mumbled the horrors she and his mother had gone through after Diego had burst into their home.

Sophia's crying was interrupted when a male nurse stepped in and informed them he was there to take her back to X-ray.

His sister gathered herself and wiped her eyes with her right hand. He noticed she hardly moved her left one and was worried suddenly that she had broken it.

Standing behind the wall and watching the image of her very broken bone appear on the computer screen, he felt the urge to kill his father. So much anger boiled in his gut that the nurse touched his shoulder.

"You're going to scare her," he said, nodding towards Sophia, who was lying in the next room, holding still for the images.

Lucas took a deep breath and tried to release his anger. "Right." He took several deep breaths.

"I took X-rays of your mother before this. She has two broken ribs. They'll want to keep her overnight. I'm sure your sister can go home tonight."

"Thanks." He worried more for his mother now.

"That's it for you," the man said cheerfully to Sophia. "I'm going to take you back so you can pick out a color for your cast."

"It's broken?" Sophia asked.

Lucas nodded. "Looks like a clean break," he said, touching her cheek. "Your head appeared broken too. He couldn't find a brain in there." He motioned to the nurse, who chuckled.

"No brain, but that means you don't have a concussion." He winked at Sophia, who smiled weakly.

The nurse touched his shoulder and nodded at him when they returned to the same room they'd been in before.

"You okay?" Sophia asked Lucas when they were alone.

"Me?" He sat on the side of her bed. "Yeah."

Sophia reached over with her right hand and touched his lips. "You have a fat lip and a black eye."

"So do you," he said with a slight frown.

"He... he tried to get me alone. Mom fought him off." Sophia looked down at her hands. "I think he wanted to—"

"Stop." he begged. "I don't know if... I want to kill the man." He stood up and ran his hands through his hair, pacing in the small space. "Shit, I wasn't there to protect you. I didn't think he'd..." He turned when the curtain opened, and Avery stepped in to wrap her arms around him.

"Your mother is being admitted and taken up to a room. Your grandfather and a man named Graig are with her now. Your mom and Graig seem... close."

"Good." He relaxed slightly. "Graig's a good man."

Avery nodded. "Yeah, I can tell. He was worried sick about you too." She turned to Sophia. "We can head up to your mother's room once they're done in here. I heard you're going to get a cast on?"

Avery released him and walked over to sit next to his sister, who looked pale and sick.

"Yeah," Sophia nodded.

"What color are you going to choose?" Avery asked as if it was a privilege to get a cast instead of a bad thing because a worse thing had happened to her.

"Blue," Sophia said, her eyes locked on his. "My brother's favorite color." She smiled a little at him.

He nodded. "I'll be back. Can you stay with her until..."

Avery nodded and touched his arm.

He nodded. "I'll be back," he told Sophia, then stepped outside.

Seeing an officer in the hallway, he marched towards the man to ask what had happened to his father.

When he stepped back into the small space, Sophia had a new blue cast on her left arm. The nurse who had flirted with him was telling Avery all about his sister's care after her discharge.

Avery listened intently to the woman's every word and even asked questions.

When the nurse left, he walked over and wrapped his arms around Avery. "Thanks."

"So?" Sophia asked. "Where's Mom?"

"Room two-thirteen," he answered.

"Dad?" Sophia asked.

"Jail. For now. We're going to make sure he stays there."

Sophia nodded. "I want to see Mom and Graig."

"Let's go then." He held out his hand for her right one.

She moved slowly, but they made their way toward the elevators, stopping by the vending machines to get her a soda, a chocolate muffin, and a candy bar.

When the three of them stepped into his mother's room, Graig stood next to his mother, looking sick and scared. He held her hand.

His grandfather rushed over to hug Sophia, holding her as his sister cried all over again in her grandfather's arms.

His grandfather repeated that he was sorry as he cried into Sophia's hair.

"Mom." Lucas moved over to his mother's bedside and nodded at Graig.

"I'm going to go check on getting you something to drink," Graig said and then leaned in and brushed his lips gently over his mother's forehead. "I'm sorry I wasn't there for you."

His mother smiled weakly at the man. "I'm sorry I pushed you away."

Graig smiled. "I'll be back to check on you soon."

His mother nodded. When Graig stepped by, he held out his hand for him and Lucas easily shook it.

"Thanks," Graig said seriously. "For being there. I plan on being around for a while, even if your mother doesn't want me to. Even if it's just to make sure she heals quickly and stays safe."

Lucas nodded. "Thanks."

After the man left, he moved over to his mother's bedside.

"Thank you," his mother whispered. She looked pale, tired, weak, and afraid.

"He's locked up," he said to the room.

His grandfather turned to him. "For how long this time?"

"This time?" Sophia asked.

Lucas closed his eyes. "I put him away last time. I damn well can do it again."

"Lucas?" Sophia moved over to his side.

"He was..." It broke him. Again, he was forced to deal with that evil night he'd walked down the hallway to use the bathroom and caught his father doing things to his daughter that no father should. His eyes searched Sophia as he shook his head. "He should have never been allowed near you again."

"You were so young," his mother broke in softly. "We were so thankful you didn't remember. For years you went to counseling. Not once did you mention it. Not once did the counselor worry that you remembered the horrible ordeal. You'd heal, physically, and mentally. You'd never know."

"Until now," Lucas broke in.

"Until now." Sophia cried and rushed to hug him. "Mom." She reached out with her right hand. "The two of you protected me."

"Always," his mother said.

"Always," he agreed.

"Always," his grandfather added.

"What now?" Sophia asked.

"Now," his grandfather said, "the two of you come and live with me or take Graig up on his offer to stay with him."

"No," his mother said firmly. "Luc, we've been over this so many times." His mother had always called his father's father Luc, since they were both Lucas. The fact was the man was more of a father to his mother than to his dad. His mother's father had passed away when she'd been ten. The moment his mother met Diego, Lucas Marcus Rodriguez had become his mother's only father figure. His mother reached over and took Sophia's hand in hers. "We're strong. We won't let him take away our home, and Graig and I... I'm not sure of anything at this point. I need to know I can do this on my own. He's a good man but..." His mother's eyes watered and she took a breath, wincing slightly.

"Mom," Sophia said with a sigh. "I don't know if I can go back there right now."

"Tonight, Sophia is going to stay with me," Lucas broke in.

"No," Avery said, stepping forward. "Tonight she's staying with us at my place. I have an extra bed," she pointed out. "You have a mattress on the floor. We'll stop off and get anything you want at your place first."

They turned back to his mother. "Yes, go stay at Avery's for tonight. After that, we'll figure something out."

He nodded and thought about his furniture in the back of his truck. "Right," he agreed.

"I want to stay here with Mom," Sophia said.

"No, sweetie. They won't let visitors after eight," his mother explained. "Go with them. Shower, clean up, change." She touched Sophia's cheek. "I'll be here, resting. Besides, Graig works the night shift and has promised to keep checking in on me." His mother turned to him. "Go, please,"

He nodded, knowing that his mother needed to be alone and rest.

"Come on, squirt." He wrapped his arm around Sophia's shoulder. "Let's go and let Mom rest."

Sophia rushed from his arms to hug their mother gently. She whispered something into their mother's ear that made her smile and nod.

"Very proud," she replied. "I'll see you tomorrow."

The three of them left his mother and grandfather in the private hospital room. His grandfather promised to stay with their mom until he was kicked out.

They drove back to the house in silence. His sister was oddly quiet between him and Avery.

"What about the cats?" Sophia said when they were a block away from the house.

"They're welcome to come tonight," Avery said quickly.

"Thanks," Sophia whispered.

"I forgot." Avery turned to him. "While I was waiting for your mother to get out of X-ray, I called my dad and brother. They have assured me that they would have your mother's front door replaced by the time we returned. They were concerned about them and wanted you to know that if you need anything, just to ask."

Lucas felt his throat close up. He wanted to tell her thank you, but he couldn't speak so instead he nodded.

"Look, there's a new door," Sophia said when they pulled up beside his mother's car again.

"Tell your family thank you," Sophia said, hugging Avery while trying not to hit her in the face with her cast.

"You can tell them yourself tomorrow morning. They're going to meet us for breakfast at the bakery in town. It was all I could do to stop them from heading to the hospital and creating a circus." She laughed.

As they climbed out of his truck, he pulled Sophia out of his side and held onto her. "I'm sorry I wasn't here sooner."

"You tried to warn me," she said with a sigh. "I'm just thankful you stopped by."

He looked at Avery over his sister's shoulder. She was wiping her eyes and smiling at them. When he noticed there was a bruise on her cheek, he held in his rage for the man who had messed with so many of the women he loved.

And the fact was, he loved Avery. He didn't know when it had happened, but she was as much in his heart as Sophia and his mother were.

Holding out his arm, he motioned for Avery to step into the hug.

When she did, he knew that whatever happened next, there was no way in hell he'd let Diego anywhere near any of them ever again.

Chapter Seventeen

With Lucas's sister and her two cats fast asleep on the sofa bed in the living room of her cottage, Avery snuggled tight against Lucas's side.

Sophia had taken almost a full hour to shower after Avery had helped her wrap her cast in a trash bag.

Lucas had wanted to barge in there when they'd heard her crying, but Avery stopped him and held onto him while he vibrated with anger geared towards their father.

"I should have killed him," he whispered over and over.

When Sophia emerged from the bathroom, he'd held onto her for the longest time. She'd made them a pan of lasagna that she'd had in her freezer along with a loaf of Italian bread. Then to follow that up, they'd eaten the rest of her ice cream while watching reruns of *Friends* until Sophia had drifted off to sleep with both cats snuggled up tight against her.

"How will they get over this?" he whispered in the quiet room.

She shifted in the dark, leaning over him. The moonlight drifted through the windows, allowing her to see his face in the soft moonlight.

"They are stronger than you know." She met his eyes. "We are strong when there is the support and love of family. I am lucky to have such an amazing one, but yours is no less than mine. Yours is stronger in ways. Your mother is an amazing woman who raised two wonderful people after living through hell. Going through fire can be difficult but what's left behind sometimes grows stronger. Sophia is an amazing woman already. She's full of humor and light." She smiled as a tear slipped down her cheek. Lucas reached up and wiped it away, cupping her face. "You're amazing. All three"—she shook her head—"four of you."

Lucas smiled. "That man doesn't have to be blood to love my mom like a daughter."

"No, he doesn't." She leaned down and brushed her lips over his. He winced slightly thanks to his cut lip, which she had cleaned earlier. "Sorry," she mumbled.

"Later, when my sister isn't just outside the bedroom door and when I won't split my lip open, I'd like to thank you properly for taking care of them." His hands moved over her body and she melted back down next to him, resting her head on his shoulders.

"I'd like that. For now, I'm too tired and a little sore to move again until morning." She fell fast asleep as he ran his fingers through her hair.

Walking into Sara's Nook the next morning to see her entire family and a few other friends gathered to support Lucas and Sophia warmed her heart. For the first few moments, Sophia appeared intimidated. Then Parker and Sara's kids, Ethan and Ellie, started running around, and Sophia easily chased after the kids, enjoying playing with them while they waited for their food.

"If you ever need a babysitter," Lucas joked to Parker.

"We'd love it." Parker laughed. "There are a handful of us that could use a good one in town. MaryBeth graduated last year and left Pride hurting for a full-time babysitter who isn't a grandparent. Also, you've taken one of our best babysitters away." He motioned to Avery with a smile. "Giving her a full-time job." He shook his head. "Are your mother and sister thinking of moving to Pride?"

Lucas shrugged. "Trust me, I'll be working to get them to agree to move closer after this. My mother is pretty stubborn. She loves her home and has worked very hard to pay it off over the years."

"Well, if she does want to sell and buy in Pride, have her call me," Hannah suggested. "We have a beautiful home in Hidden Cove that some buyers backed out of that's move-in ready. It's a three-bedroom and backs the inlet."

"I'll let her know," Lucas agreed.

"Can we see it?" Sophia said, sitting back down just as their food arrived.

"Sure." Hannah smiled. "If you want, you can follow me from here, and I can let you walk through it. Your mom can come later, once she's back on her feet."

"Thanks," Sophia said with a slight smile. Then she turned to Lucas. "I don't want to stay at that house again. I don't think..." She shook her head. "I can't."

Lucas reached over and took his sister's hand in his own. "We'll talk to Mom together. Besides, I was hoping she would stop working two jobs in town and come work for me when we opened."

Sophia's smile grew. "Seriously? She'd love that. If we lived closer, she could. I can too. I'll bus tables or wash dishes, whatever."

Lucas laughed. "Hold on, we still have to convince Mom, and she has to have time to heal."

"I'm going to stay with Grandpa. I was going to tell her this morning. I don't want to sleep in the same place I was afraid..." She dropped off and glanced over at the kids who were now eating breakfast at the next table.

"You're welcome to stay with me," Avery suggested.

"Thanks, but my grandfather has three guest rooms and I already have a bunch of my things there since I spend a lot of time watching his place when he travels," Sophia added.

"If you need anything, just text me," Avery added.

The rest of the meal was filled with talk about the kids and a birthday party they had attended the weekend before.

When they all disbursed, Lucas followed Hannah up to Hidden Cove. Avery had been in the neighborhood many times visiting Hannah and Wyatt, who now lived in a beautiful home on the hillside.

Instead of heading up the hill, Hannah turned down towards the cove area and stopped directly in front of a finished home that had a for sale sign in the yard.

"It's beautiful," Sophia said as she climbed out.

It was roughly the same size as their current place and was still a ranch-style home only with more current styling and colors. It had a massive front porch that included a porch swing.

"Here she is," Hannah said with a sigh. "I'll open her up." She headed towards the door. Sophia followed Hannah and hung on every word as she rattled off the details of the home and the neighborhood.

"Wow," Lucas said as he stepped inside. "It's nice."

"It is." Avery could just imagine Sophia's and his mother's things there. "It would be perfect for them."

"You don't know how stubborn my mother is," he said

with a sigh. "Besides, I'm not a hundred percent sure where things stand with Graig. The way the man was hovering and looking so worried about my mom, I'm sure there's something there."

"Sophia is pretty stubborn too. I'll bet you she convinces your mother to move." She walked into the kitchen area.

"I'll take that bet." Lucas held out his hand for hers. Laughing, she shook it.

"What do I win if you lose?" she asked.

His eyebrows rose. "What do I win if *you* lose?"

Just then, Sophia burst into the room, grabbed Lucas's arm with her good one, and pulled him through the rest of the house.

Avery stepped out on the back deck and looked out over the small yard and the water beyond. She couldn't help but wonder what it would be like to live there herself. She and Lucas.

"There you are," Sophia said, stepping outside. "Gosh, look at this yard and view." The girl turned to her. "It would be amazing to live here." She turned in a circle.

"Yes, it would," Avery agreed.

"If Mom doesn't go for it, Lucas should buy it. He can't live above his restaurant forever, you know." Sophia nudged her. "Like you said, his bed is on the floor." She wiggled her eyebrows.

"Not for long," Lucas said, stepping outside. "We're dropping everything off before we head to Edgeview. Parker and his crew are waiting to help us move it all upstairs. Which means, we'd better head out. Thanks for showing us the place. I'll let you know what my mother thinks."

"Sure, anytime," Hannah said as they headed out.

"Avery, I'll see you at rehearsals next week." Hannah hugged her.

"Wouldn't miss it. I've got your bachelorette party all planned out." She held in a squeal of delight.

"You're still keeping it a secret from me?" Hannah groaned.

Avery laughed and made a motion over her lips as if she were zipping them closed.

Hannah groaned and nudged her towards the door. "Go, and take your secrets with you." Her friend's laughter was intoxicating.

While she and Sophia sat in the truck, Lucas and Parker carried all of the furniture inside and up to Lucas's apartment.

"At least he won't be sleeping on a mattress on the floor any longer," Sophia said. "Still, it's a much nicer space than the last place he lived."

"Where was that?" she asked, curiously.

"He rented a small house with three other people he worked with. It was a pit," Sophia said. "His roommates were pigs."

Avery had never had a roommate. She and Hannah had planned to move in together, but the cottage only had one real bedroom. There was no way either of them were going to live on the hide-a-bed in the living room.

The ride to Edgeview was oddly quiet. At one point, Avery was convinced that Sophia had fallen asleep. Her head rested against her shoulder.

They dropped the cats back off at their house before heading to the hospital. When they parked in the hospital's parking lot, Sophia took her hand in hers.

"I don't know what I'll do if she won't agree to move out of that house," Sophia said.

"Even living with Graig and his daughter in their small apartment would be better than going back there."

"We'll convince her to do something different together," Lucas said as he took his sister's hand.

Sophia wanted to stop at the gift shop and buy their mother a bouquet.

When they walked into his mother's room, Lucas holding the flowers in his hands, his mother was already dressed and sitting on the side of the bed.

"Where do you think you're going?" Lucas asked, moving forward.

"Home," his mother answered. "They've released me. I was just waiting for you to get here."

"I don't want to go back to that place," Sophia said, rushing to her mother's side.

"Sweetie, I can't afford for us to move right now," Emily said with a soft sigh as she held her sides. "Besides, I've been assured that Diego is being transported to the county jail and that his bond will be denied. He won't be getting out anytime soon."

Avery could see that her mother's words didn't soothe Sophia any.

As she watched the family together, she wondered what she would do in Sophia's place. She'd been a teenage girl once, afraid of many things. But to find out at the tender age of sixteen that monsters were real and, more importantly, they were related to you...

She couldn't keep that thought from her head as they helped Emily out of the hospital and into the truck. When they parked at the house, she felt Sophia sag her shoulders in defeat.

Reaching over, she took her hand and squeezed it lightly.

"We'll stay for lunch," Lucas said as he helped his

mother out of the truck. "I'll make your favorite," he told Sophia with a wink.

Sophia seemed to perk up a little. Still, the moment they entered the house, even with the cats wrapping themselves around her feet, Sophia seemed nervous.

She kept glancing back toward her mother's room, where her father had abused them for hours. Threatened them. Tried to...

"What do you say we make lunch?" Avery suggested to Sophia when Lucas went back to clean the mess that was their mother's room. Emily was resting on the sofa, sleeping peacefully.

Sophia shook her head. "No, I should go help."

Avery took her hand and held onto it. "No, this your brother can do alone."

Sophia nodded. "Fine. But I've never made chicken tacos without Lucas's help. He makes the best."

"Yes, he does, but I'm pretty good at making peanut butter and jelly sandwiches," she joked.

In the kitchen, she found the ingredients for turkey sandwiches and some cans of soup. Sophia sat at the table while she prepared the meal, watching videos on her phone while the cats snuggled in her lap.

"You have a talent for making those videos, you know," she said as she worked. "Everyone in Pride is hooked on them."

Sophia glanced up and instead of lighting up like she had before when they'd talked about her videos, Sophia looked sad.

"He broke my camera." She ran her hands over the cat's fur.

Avery stilled. "I'll buy you a new one."

Sophia glanced up at her. "They're hundreds of dollars. I saved up for a whole year—"

"So," she interrupted with a shrug. "It's done. We'll head to the mall after lunch." She turned around and continued working.

She was surprised when Sophia rushed over and wrapped her arms around her from behind.

"Thank you. For everything," she said into her back.

She turned in the girl's arms and held onto her for a moment. When Lucas walked in, they were enjoying their lunch, heads bent close together as they scrolled through Sophia's phone, looking for the right camera.

The short trip to the mall while Lucas watched over his sleeping mother was one of the best girl-shopping trips Avery'd had without her besties. Shopping with a teenager was different, fun, and expensive. In the end, Sophia's new camera hadn't set her back all that much. The stores in the mall hadn't had what she'd wanted, and they'd stopped by a pawn shop on the way back home and found the perfect camera setup for Sophia and her new adventures.

The young girl was so happy, Avery's own heart filled at seeing her joy.

Chapter Eighteen

Over the next couple of days, Lucas stuck close to his family. After taking Avery back to Pride, he returned to his mom's place and spent a couple of nights in his old bedroom.

He wanted to spend the night with Avery again, but he knew she had things to tend to for Wyatt and Hannah's wedding that next weekend.

Graig kept stopping by and things were growing awkward watching the man and his mother now that they'd decided to try and make their relationship work again. He liked that the man watched over his mom and Sophia, but with the guy's hours and his duties with his daughter, he knew neither of them could watch his family full time.

He'd planned on only spending one night at his mother's place, but in the end, he stayed for two nights.

It didn't surprise him when his sister insisted they stay up all night to watch movies in the living room both nights.

He suggested that she switch her bedroom with his old one for a change, but she rejected the idea and kept trying to persuade their mother to sell the house and move to Pride.

When he returned home, he missed his time with Sophia. He desperately wished that his mother would at least consider buying the place in Pride, even if things started going well with Graig.

He drove by the little home again and even had Hannah let him inside once more.

"Just make an offer," Hannah said. "I'm sure they'll accept it. You know Todd Jordan owns all of this. He likes you, likes taking care of those who own businesses in town."

Yeah, he knew Todd Jordan. He'd met the man and his family a few times in town. Todd had made a point to welcome him to town and told him to let him know if there was anything he ever needed. The man's sister was the mayor of Pride.

He knew without a doubt that if he made an offer on the home, Todd would accept it. But this place wasn't for him. It was to be for his mother and Sophia. Wasn't it?

The more he thought about the home, the more he could see himself having a life there. A life with Avery.

Since Avery had the day off work, he spent his time training some of the new hires, including Rico, who was shaping up to be a perfect floor manager.

The sign was being installed out front but until his grand opening, which was set for the Tuesday after Wyatt and Hannah's wedding, he wanted the name he'd chosen to remain a mystery. There was a thick dark film over the square sign that held the lettering and the logo his sister had helped him come up with.

He itched to see the sign up in its full glory but knew it would be worth the wait and the added excitement for the townspeople to hold off on the unveiling.

His mother had yet to return to work due to her injuries, and Sophia wasn't returning to school for another few weeks. He was surprised when the pair of them walked in halfway through the day.

"This is a surprise." He kissed both of them. "What brings you down my way?"

"I convinced Mom to let me drive her down here to look at the house," Sophia answered excitedly.

He wouldn't admit it but a pang of jealousy hit him square in the heart. He'd started thinking about making an offer on the home himself. Even with his furniture upstairs in the apartment, his sister had been correct. It wasn't the home he envisioned raising a family in.

"That's good." He helped his mother sit down on one of the bar stools he'd purchased on his third trip to Ruby's antique shop with Avery.

"You've done wonders with this place," his mother said after sitting down. "I'm so very proud of you."

"Thanks." He sat down next to her. "You're getting some color back. Your bruising is lightening up." He touched her face.

She chuckled. "Thanks to makeup. You still look like you went toe to toe in the ring."

He chuckled. "Oh on that note, did I tell you that I met Reece Crawford? His sister is Hannah, Avery's brother Wyatt's fiancée." He took a deep breath. "Anyway, he lives in Pride."

His mother was a huge boxing fan. They'd had a cookout to watch Reece's big fight in Vegas the year before. The one where he'd been shot after he'd taken the title.

"I knew he lived in Pride," his mother said. "Did you get his autograph for me?"

He chuckled. "No, but he did promise to be here on opening day. So you can ask him for one personally."

His mother's face turned a slight pink. "He's very handsome."

Lucas laughed. "Not to mention half your age and happily married now. How are you and Graig doing?" he teased. His mother waved her hand.

"He wants us to move in together." She glanced around. "Speaking of, where's Avery? I was hoping to thank her for everything she and her family did for us."

"She has the day off. But if I know her, she'll drop by at least once sometime today. I think she's become addicted to this place."

"More like she's addicted to you." Sophia laughed.

"I can take a break and go see the house with you?" he suggested.

"We were hoping you'd come along," Sophia said, leaning on his shoulder.

"Sure, let me just tell Rico I'll be back in an hour. We can stop and grab lunch while we're out." He disappeared to find Rico entering all of the menu items into the sales system.

He'd printed off a menu while they waited for the official ones to be delivered from the printing company. Rico volunteered to enter each item and their prices into the new system Josh Williams had set up. There were touchscreen computers and printers behind the bar and at the two wait stations. However, since it was easier for Rico to enter all of the items using Avery's computer system, he sat at her desk while she was out for the day.

He looked like a giant in a dollhouse, sitting behind the desk.

"Hey, I'm going to head out for an hour with the family. You got things here?" he asked.

"Sure thing, boss." Rico smiled up at him. "Are they done hanging the sign yet?"

"No, they said another hour. They're having to rewire it and change out the fuses after they get it connected up there."

"Can't wait." Rico wiggled his eyes. "It's going to be nice knowing where my paychecks are coming from instead of just your name on them."

Lucas laughed. "What's wrong with my name?"

"Not enough flair," Rico joked.

Lucas rode in the back of his mother's car while his sister drove them the short distance to Hidden Cove.

This time, besides meeting Hannah at the house, they followed her up the hill and allowed her to show them the entire facility. The clubhouse, pools, changing rooms, and bathrooms. The tennis and pickleball courts. She had a map of the entire neighborhood and the pathways that surrounded it for hiking or biking.

There was more to Hidden Cove than he'd known about, and now he desperately wished he could move there himself.

When his mother still didn't seem interested, Hannah stepped up her game and showed her the potential sales price she could get for her home in Edgeview. That seemed to do the trick, except his mother didn't want to be down near the water. They walked up the street to a different home. It had four bedrooms and another room that could be used as an office.

His mother and Sophia instantly fell in love with the home. When she mentioned that there would be enough room for Graig and his daughter, he understood what was going on and was very happy that they had decided to make the big change.

She put an official offer on the place, subject to her house in Edgeview selling. This home was still being built, which meant they couldn't move in for a few months. That gave her plenty of time to sell her place and for Graig's lease on his apartment to run out.

All of this took a lot longer than an hour, which meant that he'd made three calls to the restaurant. Every time, Rico told him to take his time and assured him that everything was under control.

They were just about to leave when he asked about making an offer on the other place.

Hannah smiled and told her that she'd talked to Todd already.

"He says make him an offer. Just so we're clear, there's no possibility of personalization any longer. The house is complete."

"I like the place as is," he answered. "How about twenty thousand under asking?"

Hannah leaned closer to him and whispered, "Welcome to the neighborhood." She held out her hand to him. "I'll draw up the contract and email it to you this afternoon." She gripped his hand a little firmer and leaned in again. "Oh, and if you hurt Avery in any way"—her eyes narrowed—"I'll know just where to find you."

He chuckled. "Gotcha. You have officially scared me."

Hannah shook her head and smiled. "You should be very afraid."

"With friends like this, I know she's worth the fight."

"Good answer." Hannah winked at him. "Now, go have lunch with your family. Your sister looks like she's about to expire from starvation."

After lunch, his mother and sister headed back to Edgeview. By the time he made it back to his place, the sign was completed and the construction crew was gone.

The moment he stepped out onto the sidewalk to appreciate it, several people walked over to chat with him, trying to get him to divulge the name.

While he stood there and joked with them, he began to feel what it was like to be an insider. To be one of the townspeople. Everyone knew him by name. Knew his story. Asked after his mom and sister.

Since he wanted to know more people, he asked about each one of them and mentally made notes for future run-ins.

This was what it was to be a business owner in a small town, something he'd dreamed about his entire life.

He'd never imagined he'd come this far. To own his very own restaurant, and now, it appeared, to possibly own a home too. Of course, there was still the nasty bit about getting approved for a loan for the home and coming up with the down payment. But he figured he could deal with that after the wedding next weekend. He might just make enough to start the process.

With a smile on his lips, he stepped through his front doors and stopped dead in his tracks. There, standing at the brightly colored bar, was his father, leaning against it as if he owned the place.

"What in the hell." He rushed towards the man but stopped dead in his tracks when a man in a suit stepped in front of him.

"Mr. Jenkins? Lucas Jenkins?" the man asked while his father sneered at him.

"Yes," he said, not taking his eyes off his old man.

"You've been served." The man held up a large envelope for Lucas.

"Fine, now get the hell off my property," he barked, taking the envelope from the man.

"Not yours for long, boy." His father laughed as he and the man walked out of the room.

He wanted to tear the envelope up, but he locked the front door and sat at the bar to open it.

"What's that, boss?" Rico asked as he came out of the office.

"My father is trying to sue me," he said, still reading the fine print.

"I thought you said your old man was in jail and was going to be there for a long time?" Rico sat next to him.

"I thought that up until the moment I found him leaning on this very bar not two minutes ago."

"Shit, that was him? The pair of them came in and asked if they could wait for you to get back. I was just getting my cell phone to give you a call and let you know they were here," Rico answered, waving his phone. "What does it say?" He asked, looking over his shoulder.

"He's trying to pin some of his crimes on me and claiming I'm financially responsible for the injuries that he suffered when I attacked him. He's listed this place as an asset he is seeking to gain control over." He slammed the paper down. "He held my mother and sister prisoner in their own home and wants me to pay for it?" He pulled out his phone and the card from the detective in charge of his mother's case. Why in the hell hadn't he been told his father was out of jail already? The last he'd heard, the man was being transported and had been denied bond.

His blood turned ice-cold as he thought of his mom and sister. He hung up just as the phone rang once to the detective and quickly called his mother.

"He's out," he said when she answered.

"What?" His mother's voice dipped.

"Dad. He was just here. He's suing me for this place. You and Sophia turn back around and get over here. You're staying with me until..."

"No, honey, I... I don't think..." His mother started crying. "Your place is not big enough. We don't have any of our clothes. The cats."

"I'll head to town after you're here and get everything you need. You'll stay at Avery's place. She can stay here with me. Just get back here. I'll make it work. Just... turn around now."

"Okay, okay." His mother hung up.

He called Avery and quickly told her what was happening.

"I'll make sure my place is ready for them. They can stay there as long as they need. I'll pack a bag and meet you over there," she said before hanging up.

"Looks like you just moved in together." Rico slapped him on the back. "Let me know if you need me for anything. Now that I know what the man looks like, he'll never step foot in here again," he assured Lucas.

"Thanks." Lucas shook the man's hand.

A few minutes before Avery arrived with two bags of her things, George Stevens, his cousin Robin's husband, knocked on the glass doors.

"Avery called me. I heard you might need me to look over some papers?" George said with a smile.

George's law offices were just down the street. He could see them if he leaned out the front door. He hadn't even thought to give the man a call.

As the man sat in one of his new booths, looking over the paperwork, Avery made them all some iced coffee.

"Well?" he asked when George was done reading.

He laughed. "The man's lawyer is an idiot. There is no way this is going to stand up. First, I did some checking on your father before I headed over here. He's out on a temporary bond with a restraining order and a no-contact order."

"So he's broken that already by coming here?" Lucas asked.

George shook his head. "You were not listed on the restraining order. Just your mother and sister."

"He also has regular check-ins, which I can check to see if he's good on first thing in the morning." George wrote something down. "I'll take these with me." He stopped. "That is assuming you want to hire me?"

"Yes, please. I have no idea where to start."

George smiled. "This is a good start, hiring me. Don't worry, I'll give you the family rate." He winked. "Or I could trade for free tacos for life."

Lucas chuckled then added. "Could you help file a restraining order for me? I don't ever want that man on my property again."

"Sure thing. I'll post it in the morning." George stood up. "We all can't wait for this place to open. Don't worry," he said as he shook his hand. "He's punching out to draw blood when he couldn't get it from your mom and sister. Trust me, we'll put this man where he belongs." He shook his hand and then left.

Avery walked into his arms and held onto him when they were alone. He had everything he needed, right here, to get him through what was going to happen next.

She'd been right, his mother and sister were strong enough to fight against the man. Now it was his turn and, this time, he wasn't using fists. This time, he'd go back to using the law.

Chapter Nineteen

very was very thankful that she was going to be back in Lucas's arms. Even if it was under stressful circumstances, it felt so right.

"Stop thinking about it," she said, pulling away from him and looking up into his eyes. "George knows what he's doing. Trust me."

He nodded once quickly. "What now?"

He'd just returned from Edgeview after gathering the cats and everything his mother and sister would need for a few days.

"Now you help me move my bags upstairs." She smiled. "Then we can cook for your family so they have a good meal before we take them over to the cottage and get them settled in."

"Okay." He took her hand in his, then leaned down and brushed his lips across hers. "Thank you for this."

"Any time." She smiled and followed him into the kitchen.

She helped him prepare a smaller meal just for the four of them. When his mother and sister knocked on the back door, she let them in. Instead of sitting out in the dining room, they took their food out to the patio area and ate under the new string lights.

"We won't have many quiet nights like this soon," Lucas said, leaning back in his chair.

"It will be wonderful," his mother replied.

"I wish we could move into the house tonight," Sophia added.

"You're welcome to stay at my place until then," Avery offered. "Just as long as your brother allows me to stay with him." She smiled.

Lucas took her hand and lifted it to his lips. "As long as you want, you're welcome."

She felt her stomach flutter at the simple touch. Since the other night, she'd replayed the night over and over in her head. How tender he was. How much she wanted him to touch her again.

"On that note." Sophia sat up a little. "I think I can get us to the cottage." She stood up. "Keys?" She held her hand out to Avery, who laughed and handed them over. "Rusty and Luna are tired and want to get out of their carriers." She motioned to the two cats, who were sleeping peacefully beside them.

"If you need anything," Avery started.

"You've done enough." Emily touched her shoulder, then leaned down and planted a kiss on her cheek. "Thank you. Goodnight." She kissed Lucas and then started to lift one of the cats, but Lucas jumped up and carried both of the carriers to his mother's car.

Seeing Sophia drive them away, Avery relaxed. Then Lucas came back and pulled her to her feet and led her inside.

"What about the dishes?" She laughed.

"Later," he said with a smile. "For now, I think it's only fair that I properly thank you." They stepped inside and suddenly her back was against the wall as his mouth covered hers.

Passion. Need. Heat.

There was so much of it, she became breathless as her head spun and her desire spiked.

"I'll lock up," he said against her lips.

"I'll take the front door; you take the back." She ducked under his arms and rushed through the building to flip the front door locks.

They met back at the staircase, their bodies slamming into one another. Her hands moved to his hair as she jumped up and wrapped her legs around him.

"My god," he groaned as he fumbled to open the door to the stairs. "I can't seem to move fast enough."

She laughed as he almost dropped her on the staircase.

"Hurry." She trailed her mouth over his neck. "Hurry," she said again when they reached the top.

She didn't realize they'd made it to the bedroom until her back hit the mattress. He must have set his bed up fully because it was no longer on the ground.

"Thank god you fixed the bed." She started pulling her jeans off her legs.

He nodded and cursed under his breath when she fought the zipper on his pants.

"Too many damned clothes," he groaned as she kicked off her sandals so he could pull her pants the rest of the way off her legs.

"Next time, we start this naked." She laughed as he jerked his shirt over his head.

She flipped hers off and tossed it across the room, then knelt on the bed in her panties and bra as he finished removing his jeans. When he knelt beside her, pulling her body against his, she knew that she'd never tire of the feeling of him.

"This will never get old," she groaned as he traced her neckline with his tongue.

"I need to be inside you now. We can go slow and enjoy one another later." He dipped a finger under her panties and slipped into her heat smoothly.

"Yes," she cried out and arched into his touch. "Please," she begged as she reached out and took him in her hand.

"I swear we'll go slower next time." He reached away from her to grab a condom from his nightstand.

Then he was back, nudging her shoulders onto the bed and covering her.

She couldn't remember feeling anything this strong before. The desire was going to make her burst if he didn't touch her again. If he didn't kiss her again soon.

Wrapping her legs around his hips, she held on as he claimed her once more. He took what he wanted and at the same time gave her the world.

"We should have won some sort of award just now," she said a little breathless. Their bodies were covered in a layer of sweat as they lay on his bed looking up at the ceiling.

"Speed fucking." He laughed. "It's a sport. I think."

She laughed and rolled towards him. "We can go for the slow award later. Right now, I think I want a shower."

"Ditto." He rolled towards her until they were face to face.

She watched his eyes move over her face, dip to her lips, and back to her eyes. Instantly, she could tell he wanted her again.

"Keep that up and we might not make it to the shower." She touched his cheek.

"Everything is happening so quickly," he said as he closed his eyes.

"We did just claim an award for that, right?" she joked.

He smiled and looked at her. "The business, us, everything with my... Diego." He took a deep breath. "Oh, I almost forgot. Mom and Sophia told you about putting an offer on the cottage, but I forgot to mention that I put an offer on the place on the inlet the other day."

She smiled. "Hannah told me. She called me seconds after you left." She shrugged. "I figured you'd tell me when you wanted to."

He nodded and rolled towards her again, touching her face gently. "So much has happened since we were here last."

She smiled. "Bad and good."

His smile slipped a little. "Sorry about the bad."

"The good has far outshined the bad." She leaned in and kissed him. "Like tonight."

He nodded. "That shower," he said against her lips, "is going to have to wait."

The next few days flew by so quickly that the only thing Avery remembered were the long nights in Lucas's arms and hanging out with Sophia and Emily each day at work.

Sophia helped her get a few more details together for Hannah's bachelorette party and even helped decorate that morning.

After donning the dress she'd picked out to wear to the rehearsal and the dinner following, she left Lucas and headed over to Sunset Venue.

Seeing her best friend and her brother stroll into the place where they would be married the following day had tears rolling down her cheeks.

She rushed to hug them both and ended up making Hannah cry as well.

"I'm sorry," she kept saying as she laughed and tried to wipe the tears from her friend's eyes before she ruined her makeup.

"It's too late. We're both ruined." Hannah laughed. "Bathroom break," she told Wyatt, who nodded as he rolled his eyes.

Avery reached over and slugged him on the shoulder. "Go tell everyone inside we need a moment." She shoved her brother, took Hannah's hand, and led her around the side to the bathrooms.

"Sisters," she said once they were inside, and hugged Hannah again.

"Sisters. Finally." Hannah hugged her back.

Once their makeup was back in place, they strolled into the barn arm-in-arm.

Wyatt immediately took Hannah from her, and Avery stepped up to do her maid of honor duties. She'd be there, as promised, first thing in the morning to help oversee the final details of all the decorations and to deliver the bridesmaids' dresses and shoes, and the gifts that she had helped Hannah put together for her other bridesmaids. Hannah wouldn't let Avery see her gift, but she had an idea of what she would be getting.

For her part, Avery had put a lot of time and money into plotting out the most amazing, unique gift ever. She had wanted something that both Wyatt and Hannah could enjoy for years to come.

Her gift wouldn't technically arrive until the morning, but she'd made a point to have everything in order.

Watching the happy couple walk through their rehearsal had her mind turning to her possibilities. Lucas.

In the short months they'd known one another, she'd grown closer to him than anyone before. The way he took care of his mother and sister told her what kind of man he was. The man he would always be.

She'd seen his temper towards his father. But he'd turn it off when she or his mother or sister got near him. Avery knew that it was so he didn't scare them. He cared so much that he could instantly shift his feelings so as not to hurt theirs.

The amount of control it took him impressed her. She hated Diego for what he'd done to the family. She'd only seen him that one time, but Lucas had urged her to run or call the police if she ever ran into him again. What she wanted to do was use some of those self-defense skills Reece had taught her.

After the rehearsal, everyone headed to the Golden Oar. The entire outside deck had been booked for the private dinner.

She sat next to Hannah and her brother with the rest of the family and ate dinner, looking out at the Pacific Ocean while the sun sank. The moment the string lights overhead flickered on and Hannah was done with dinner, she grabbed her hand and pulled her up.

"Well, this has been fun, but me and the other bridesmaids"—she nodded towards Brook and Kate—"are going to kidnap the bride." She glanced over to Reece and Tom. "I suggest you men take my brother and do whatever you're going to do to him." She winked at Wyatt before tugging on Hannah's arm. She was pulled to a stop when Hannah leaned in and placed a very passionate kiss on her brother's lips. The entire group cheered and egged them on until Avery tugged once more on Hannah's arm and broke them free.

"Where are we going?" Hannah asked after the four of them were crammed into Avery's car.

"It's a surprise," she said, laughing.

"I'm tired," Hannah started. "And I have to be up—"

"Don't start with me," Avery said in a firm voice. "We are going to party like it's the last night of your single life."

Hannah and her other friends laughed.

Chapter Twenty

Why had he agreed to host a party the night before a big job?

Lucas stood behind the DJ table watching Avery and almost a dozen of her girlfriends dance around the patio, bumping to the music as if they were in a Las Vegas nightclub instead of his newly redesigned patio area. The string lights overhead and the disco ball and strobe lights that Avery had set up made the small space seem like a nightclub.

She'd hired one of her friends to DJ the event and had even set up the karaoke machine. He and his kitchen staff had made small appetizers and specialty drinks for the event.

Avery had been able to get his liquor license pushed through thanks to her contacts at the city building, so his new bartender, Yolanda, was working overtime to keep up with the group of women.

At one point, Avery tried to pull him out onto the dance floor, but instead, he pulled her back into the hallway and kissed her until they were both breathless.

When she tried to get him to dance with her after, he'd pointed out that it wouldn't be fair to the other ladies, since he'd be the only man on the floor.

She laughed and just then Hannah had rushed in and pulled her back outside before he could change his mind and convince her to skip the party and head upstairs instead.

An hour after they'd arrived, Wyatt and the entire bachelor party joined the group. He didn't know if they'd just stumbled upon the party or if someone had invited them. Either way, he was thankful since it gave him and his staff the opportunity for a dry run the following evening.

This time when Avery tried to pull him out for a dance, he willingly went since the floor was filled with other couples.

"Thank you," Avery whispered.

"For?" he asked, holding her closer and enjoying the way her body fit next to his.

The little strapless dress she'd worn that evening clung to her and he was thankful he'd gotten plenty of opportunities to watch her move in it. He wanted her and knew that, after everyone left, they'd head upstairs and he'd get to enjoy her once more.

"Everything." She glanced up at him with a grin.

He chuckled. "Enjoying yourself?"

She nodded and then glanced over at Hannah and her brother. "They're happy," she said with a sigh.

He nodded. "You throw a wonderful party."

She shook her head. "If not for you, I'd be having this party at a pizzeria." She laughed. "This is so much more amazing. Everyone in town will want to rent this space out for summer dance parties. We'll have to come up with other plans during the winter."

He nodded. "I was thinking about gutting the upstairs and making it more space for the restaurant."

"That is an amazing idea." He chuckled and caught her from tumbling over. "Thank you for tonight," she said again and rested her head on his shoulder.

"Any time." He held her until the song ended.

Less than an hour later, everyone shuffled into cars and headed home. He was thankful there were a few designated drivers in the mix to ensure that everyone got home safely.

Leaving Rico and his other staff members to clean and lock up downstairs, he helped Avery up to their apartment.

"I like staying here," she said as she slipped off her shoes. "I'm going to miss it when your mom and Sophia move into their new place."

"If the paperwork goes through, I won't be staying here much longer. My closing is set for a month from now," he pointed out. "You could always just stay here with me?" He held his breath.

She tilted her head and sat on the edge of the bed.

"Lucas Jenkins, are you asking me to move in with you?"

He laughed and, with great fanfare, he knelt at her feet and took her hands into his. "Avery Auston, will you officially move in with me?"

She laughed and wrapped her arms around his shoulders. "Yes," she said before kissing him.

"Avery," he said softly against her skin. "Since the moment calls for it, I'll tell you." He pulled back and looked into her eyes. "I think I've fallen in love with you."

Her smile doubled. "Good, because I *know* I have fallen in love with you."

He chuckled and kissed her as he nudged her back onto the bed and covered her with his body.

His hands ran up her thighs, nudging the silky dress up higher until he exposed those pretty cream-colored panties she'd put on before leaving. Since the dress was strapless, she'd skipped the matching bar and he was thankful for that when he slipped her breast out to suck on it.

Her hands were buried in his hair as she moaned and wrapped her legs tight around him. She moved her hips, swaying against him until he was so hard that he grew uncomfortable in his jeans.

He slipped them off, and when he slid into her, she moaned his name and then whispered, "I love you," against his ear. Those simple words triggered a primal instinct to claim what was his, and his body took over completely.

Avery met each of his movements with demands of her own. When they were both sated, they fell asleep in each other's arms.

The alarm woke him earlier than he'd wished. Avery, who had been wrapped around him, groaned softly, then jolted awake and sat straight up.

"Today's the day!" she said with excitement.

"It is." He rolled over to cover his head with the blankets.

Avery pulled them off his head. "Today. Is. The. Day." She said, smiling. "I'm finally getting a sister."

He chuckled and tried to pull her back down into bed with him. She was too fast and dodged his hands.

He closed his eyes and rolled back over, tucking himself under the blankets. When he heard the shower running and Avery singing, he smiled and knew that he'd better get up and prepare for the long day ahead.

The wedding was at three, which meant that he had plenty of time to haul everything he and his new crew needed over to his cousins' place. Still, he'd promised Avery he'd help her take everything she needed over first. If she was up this early, he'd better get moving.

Besides, he was thinking about sneaking into the shower with her and distracting her for a while.

By the time he made it into the bathroom, though, she was already out, a towel wrapped around her body and one around her long hair.

"I wasn't quick enough." He pulled her into his arms and kissed her.

"No, you weren't. But you are just in time to get in that shower." She yanked down his boxer shorts and left him standing in the middle of the bathroom, laughing. "Hurry up," she called after him when he stepped into the hot shower.

By the time he was done, she was dressed in a pair of cream-colored yoga pants and a tank top. Her long wet hair was piled on top of her head in one of the caps she wore that would end up making her hair curly after it dried.

Even without any makeup, dressed like that, she still managed to take his breath away.

With a towel wrapped around his hips, he pulled her into a hug and kissed her.

"Today is going to be amazing," he promised her. "You have me until around eleven. What do you need of me?"

She smiled up at him. "First, get dressed. Second, help me find my phone." She threw up her hands. "I can't find it anywhere."

"It's probably downstairs still. We came up in sort of a hurry," he said, moving the pillows aside.

"Can you call it?"

He walked over and hit dial, and heard her phone ring from somewhere in the room.

Avery rushed around and finally found it behind the

nightstand. "I've missed three calls already." She sat on the edge of the bed and called Hannah.

He listened to their quick conversation, gathering that Avery needed to stop off somewhere along the way to the venue.

Less than half an hour later, after a very rushed breakfast of toast and orange juice, they headed out.

They picked up the bridesmaid dresses and gifts from Hannah's parents' place. He had followed her and helped carefully store them all in the back of her car.

All of the cooking equipment he'd need for the day along with most of the ingredients were packed away in his truck. He'd no doubt make several trips during the next few hours, but it was a start.

He could also have Rico or Yolanda bring anything else that was needed.

He helped her cart everything in, including a large box of carefully wrapped gifts that were tucked into soft teal bags. She'd told him they were for the bridesmaids and groomsmen.

With Avery's help, he'd picked out a unique gift for the couple at Ruby's the last time they'd been there. The gold-plated mirror was antique and elegant style was something he could see Hannah and Wyatt enjoying. Avery had helped him secure it in a box and wrap it in soft blue wrapping paper with little bells on it.

Since he hadn't known what to say on the card, he'd just signed his name. He had strict orders to deliver the mirror to the present table, which would be set opposite the cake table, shortly before the wedding, which was to be held out on the beach just outside of the barn venue. Until then, the mirror sat securely in the back seat of his truck.

After helping Avery carry in the last load of her things,

he glanced down at his watch and was surprised that it was a quarter to eleven already.

He kissed her goodbye and left her to start hauling his things inside while she went to get ready with the rest of her friends, whom he'd seen arrive shortly after they'd gotten there.

Hannah wasn't in that group, but he figured she was already inside somewhere.

Taking the first load of things he'd need, Lucas disappeared into the kitchen, ready to get to work. An hour later, he was helping Rico carry in the rest of the supplies.

For the next few hours, his main focus was food. He glanced up once to chat with his cousin Kara, who informed him that Robin was in labor and on her way to the hospital.

"I think she just wanted to get out of a day of work," Kara joked. "I'm going to head there as soon as I have word she's fully dilated."

"Keep me posted." He moved out of the way of one of his staff.

"I'll get out of the way. I just wanted you to know." Kara laughed. "I'm going to be an aunt finally."

After that, he went and changed into his official chef outfit. This one was for show since Hannah and Wyatt had requested that he make a few appearances throughout the evening, and he wanted to look his best. He'd purchased the black pants and chef coat specifically for the event and the opening of his place. He had purchased each of his kitchen staff their own embroidered shirts with the restaurant's name and their name on it for opening day.

"Keep an eye on the time," he called to his staff.

"Yes, chef," they replied.

He got a sense of pride just hearing that. He'd hired the best and the proof was in each dish they completed.

Less than an hour before the wedding, Avery stepped inside the door.

Seeing her in the soft teal bridesmaid dress stopped his heart. Without realizing it, he moved over towards her.

"You look..." He blinked a few times and swallowed the knot in his throat.

"I'll take your silence as a compliment." She smiled up at him.

"It is." He nodded profusely.

"I like your outfit too." She ran a finger over the black buttons on his shirt.

"Thanks." He glanced at the door. "You shouldn't be in here. You could get something on your dress."

"I just wanted to come in and see you. To tell you..." She lifted her arms over his shoulders. "I'll be thinking of you."

He smiled. His hands itched to grab her, but he was afraid he'd get her dress dirty. Instead, he balled them by his sides.

"I wish I could watch the wedding." He motioned with his head. "Lots to do still."

She nodded. "You are going to knock everyone's socks off with whatever smells so good in here." She groaned. "We should have eaten more than just toast and juice."

"Oh." He held up his hand. "I have something for that." He walked over and picked up a basket. "I made these for you, just in case you stopped by. There is extra in case you want to share." He handed her a basket. "They're conchas, also known as Mexican pan dulce. It's a sweet bread, sort of like a streusel pastry." They were perfect since there would be no mess to drop onto anyone's dress.

"These are perfect," Avery said after taking a bite. "The other girls were complaining of being hungry. I'm going to go share them now." She lifted on her toes and kissed him. "Thank you."

He nodded. "I'll see you for dinner."

She smiled and called back. "Love you."

"So..." Rico suddenly appeared by his side and slapped him on the shoulder. Hard. "You've moved into the love phase."

Lucas chuckled and told the man to get back to work.

Chapter Twenty-One

As she walked down the sandy makeshift aisle lined with white rose petals, holding a small bouquet of wildflowers, the situation hit Avery hard. Things were changing. Everything was changing.

Today, she and Hannah would finally be sisters. How long had they dreamed of this day? She was as close to Hannah as she was to Wyatt.

She and her friends had helped Hannah get ready all morning long. There had been plenty of laughter and some tears as the four of them sipped champagne and helped each other with hair and makeup.

The small gifts Hannah had given each of them, silver necklaces shaped in her favorite starfish design, were around each of their necks as they walked down the aisle. Avery's gift to Hannah and Wyatt was already set up off to the side, hidden from their view for now.

Hannah had gifted her an extra maid of honor gift of a small diamond heart bracelet. She was wearing it now and would probably never take it off ever again.

Avery stood beside Brook and Kate, and they all waited

as the music changed and Wyatt stepped to the end of the aisle. Every guest turned to watch as the music beat started to pump.

Her brother and his groomsmen, all dressed in tan suits, had everyone laughing as they danced their way down the aisle towards the flower-covered archway. Their synchronized routine had been practiced to perfection.

She was laughing so hard that her sides hurt by the time Wyatt and the others took their spots across from them.

Then the music changed once again and Hannah stepped out from behind the white tent that blocked everyone's view of her.

The front of Hannah's hair was curled and wrapped around a simple tiara, while the rest of it flowed in soft curls around her shoulders. The white spaghetti-strap dress had a corset on the upper half and a long, flowing light-as-air skirt, It was the most beautiful dress Avery had ever seen. The day she'd helped Hannah pick it out, they had both known instantly that it was the dress.

Tears blurred Avery's vision as the laughter still had her heart swelling at her stupid brother's moves. Glancing over to her brother, she saw his eyes start to water too.

Today was perfect. Her brother was marrying the woman of his dreams. She had a sister that she'd dreamed of her entire life. And, most importantly, she was in love.

She listened as Hannah and Wyatt spoke the vows they'd written for one another. Avery handed Hannah her vows in a special paper to which she'd added a light dusting of sand for Hannah's joke to Wyatt. When Hannah blew the sand off her vows, as if she'd written them long ago, everyone in the crowd laughed.

The fact that the two of them had been destined to be

together was no secret to anyone at the wedding or, for that matter, anyone in Pride.

As they kissed one another finally as a married couple, she let those tears that had been building up fall down her cheeks as she cheered. When Hannah rushed over to her and hugged her, more tears fell.

"Sisters forever," she whispered as she handed Hannah back her bouquet.

Watching the happy couple walk down the aisle, she glanced over to where her gift sat and smiled. She itched to give it to them now but knew it would be sitting right where they would see it when they walked in out of the sunlight.

Hannah and Wyatt's wedding photographer had everyone in the wedding party wait under the tent for photos while everyone else headed inside, so she wasn't there to see her gift just yet or to see everyone's reaction to it.

She grew more anxious as they spent almost half an hour taking photos on the sand.

"All done out here," the photographer finally said.

"Time to head inside." She clapped her hands and got everyone's attention. Everyone followed her back to the barn, where she'd made sure the outer doors had been shut and the happy couple would be the first to walk in.

Turning with her back to the doors, she took her brother's and sister-in-law's hands in her own.

"One of my duties as maid of honor includes making this day extremely special for both of you. To do that, I decided to roll my gift to you in with a special surprise that the two of you would cherish and be able to share with loved ones for the rest of your lives." She smiled and felt her heart flutter.

"What did you do?" Wyatt groaned, causing her to laugh.

"From me to the two of you. My brother, who was born to torture me, but who would eventually give me the sister that I deserve." She laughed and then flung open the barn doors.

Hannah and Wyatt had to blink a few times. She did as well until her eyes adjusted to the large canvas, which was set directly inside the barn doors. It was surrounded by white roses and wildflowers and sat directly under a light that highlighted the artwork.

There stood the most amazing painting of their wedding that anyone could have ever captured. Everything was so perfect, the beach beyond the floral archway looked almost alive. The wedding party stood around the bride and groom, surrounding them as Hannah and Wyatt looked lovingly into one another's eyes.

"How did you..." Hannah rushed forward, pulling Wyatt with her. "It's a painting," she exclaimed as Avery stepped inside.

"All thanks to Elle Comings." Avery took the artist's hand and pulled her closer.

"Elle?" Hannah gasped. "You're freaking famous."

Elle laughed. The woman was a young prodigy who could quickly and very accurately paint any scene. Some of her artwork rivaled that of Pride's very own Allison Jordan. Allison had been Avery's foot in the door. Elle had jumped at the chance to do the wedding after Avery had hinted that Allison and her family would be in attendance. Of course, her bill was something Avery would need to work extra hours to pay off.

"I love it." Hannah hugged Elle and then turned to Avery. "It's perfect."

"This is amazing, sis." Wyatt hugged her. "It's going to hang over our fireplace for the rest of our lives."

"Good. That's where it belongs. Now, head on inside. Your guests are waiting to eat all that amazing food my boyfriend has made for you."

Hannah chuckled and then Avery stood back as the happy couple walked around the corner to cheers from all of the guests.

"Thank you." Avery hugged Elle. "It's even more perfect than I could have imagined."

"This was such an amazing wedding. I've fallen in love with your little town," Elle said. "I may have to come back more often. The B and B you put me up in is amazing. I've arranged to stay a few more days so I can paint each colorful cabin."

"You won't be the first," she joked. "Allison is inside. Would you like me to introduce you?"

"I've already met her. When she came in with her husband, gosh, I about had a heart attack. Then she saw my painting and we chatted for the longest time. She wants me to sit at their table with them."

When they stepped into the main room, everyone clapped at Elle's amazing artwork, so Avery slipped to the side to go find Lucas. To her surprise, he was walking around the room chatting with people.

"Hey," he said, smiling when he saw her. "How did everything go?"

"Perfectly." She sighed and wrapped her arms around him. "Did you get a chance to see my gift?"

"I did." He kissed her. "She's very talented. I had a chance to talk to her about doing something for our place before she leaves town."

"Really?" Avery grew excited. Why hadn't she thought of that?

Just then, Parker interrupted them and Lucas had to go chat with someone he wanted to introduce him to. Avery made her way to her brother's side.

Wyatt wrapped his arm around her shoulders as he talked to Reece.

"Happy?" she asked when the conversation was over.

"Very." Her brother kissed her cheek. He nodded towards Lucas. "He's a hit before they even bring out the main course."

She laughed. "I have a feeling we're going to be very busy come Tuesday."

"I wish we were going to be here for your big day," Wyatt said with a grin.

"Hawaii is going to be much better," she said with a laugh. "When you get back, I'll treat you to some tacos and margaritas."

"Deal," Wyatt said and then dropped his hold on her to shake Ryder's hand.

She stood and listened to the men chat for a moment before Ryder asked her. "Is Lucas around? I have some news from George."

"Where is he?" Wyatt asked as he glanced around.

Ryder chuckled. "His wife decided that your wedding day was a perfect birthday as well."

"What?" they both said together.

"They're all at the hospital right now. But George wanted me to give Lucas some important news."

"He's..." She glanced around. "Probably back in the kitchen. I'll walk with you to the back." She led Ryder towards the kitchen. "What's the news?"

Ryder sighed. "George said that Lucas wouldn't mind if you know, so I'll tell you. They've revoked his father's bail."

"That's good news," she said, stopping outside the kitchen doors.

"It is, except they can't seem to find the man to haul him back to prison," Ryder said. "Which is why George wanted to warn Lucas."

"Yeah, that's bad news." She opened the door. The two of them stepped inside the kitchen at the same time. When Avery saw the scene inside, she gasped and then was shoved behind Ryder.

Every person in the kitchen, all of the new staff that she'd hired and Lucas, stood frozen in place. Diego stood in the middle of the room, dressed in black from head to toe, a large rifle strapped to his chest with enough ammo on the two belts wrapped around his hips to take out everyone in the entire town of Pride.

When they had stepped foot in the kitchen, Diego's head jerked towards them for a split second.

"You don't want to do this," Lucas said quickly, getting his father's attention again with his hands up in the air. He was standing so close to Diego. Too close.

Avery wanted to shout at him to back away. To run. To hide. But she was frozen in place. Frozen with fear. In all her life, she'd never imagined something like this happening.

"Tell me where they are, boy," Diego slurred. "I just want my family. I want what's mine."

"That's not going to happen," Lucas said, calmly. "They're out of your reach."

No! she wanted to shout at him. Tell him something. Anything to get him away from here. Away from the man she loved.

"You think you're so goddamned smart? You think you're better than me?" Diego shouted. "You owe me. You lied to them all those years ago and sent me away. Ten fucking years I rotted in jail. All because you lied." He jerked slightly, moving the butt of the weapon higher so that the gun was now aimed at Lucas's legs. "You owe me," he growled.

"Then take it out on me. These people"—he motioned around the room—"have nothing to do with us."

Diego seemed to realize for the first time that there were other people in the room other than Lucas. A sneer formed on his lips.

"If you don't want anyone hurt, you'd best start talking," Diego hissed as he raised the gun to Lucas's chest.

"No!" Avery shouted, stepping in front of Ryder. "I know where they are," she screamed. "I'll take you to them."

"No!" Lucas shouted.

She avoided his eyes. "They're in a cabin not far from here. It's..." She turned slightly and glanced at Ryder, locking eyes with him. "It's just a short walk from here." She tugged on Ryder's arm as the man tried to pull her backward. "I'm taking him to Robin and Kara's cottage," she hissed at Ryder. His eyes grew wide, and he nodded with understanding. "That's where Emily and your daughter are," she said to Diego. "Will you come with me?"

Diego jerked his head. "You're that bitch that was there that day with him." He nodded at Lucas.

"If you lay one finger on her..." Lucas started, but Avery jumped in.

"Yes, I was there, and I know where Emily and Sophia are." She started walking slowly towards the back door. "Follow me."

To her shock and surprise, the man did so, as if he were

in a daze. When he got closer to her, the reek of alcohol almost caused her to double over.

Before she reached the back door, Ryder was out of the kitchen, no doubt heading to get the help they needed. As she stepped out the back door, into the now cool evening air, she glanced back one last time at Lucas. His fists were balled together, and she could tell he was trying to figure out how to take out the man armed to the teeth and ready to go on a killing spree.

This was the only way she knew how to get him away from the people she loved. To sacrifice herself for the many that she loved.

Her entire life had been one big sacrifice, hadn't it? She'd jumped from job to job, all to help those in need. If it meant giving herself to save every single person in the other room, everyone in the building, in Pride, then she'd gladly do so. Even if it meant losing everything she'd recently gained. Lucas's love. Her one chance at her very own happy-ever-after. It was worth the price.

Chapter Twenty-Two

"What in the hell was she thinking?" Lucas cursed under his breath.

"We've called the police," someone said as he darted towards the door that Avery and Diego had just walked out of.

"Easy," Rico said, holding him back.

"I'm going after them," he growled.

"You and what army? Did you happen to see what the man was carrying?" Rico pointed out. "Enough firepower to take out everyone in this building, twice over."

Just then the kitchen doors burst open, and Ryder rushed back in. He'd only met the man officially a few hours before. Still, he knew instantly that the guy was a kindred spirit when he dipped into fluent Spanish with one of his staff members. "They've got this under control," he told Lucas, taking his shoulders in his hands. "Trust me on this. Half of the police department and the entire fire station were out there." He pointed behind him. "Most of them are carrying weapons themselves. They're sneaking around to the cottage and will get Avery away from him. Trust us on this. We take care of our own." Ryder shook his shoulders.

"My mom? Sister?" he asked, his ears ringing oddly.

"Aiden is sending someone over to Avery's place to check up on them now. From the sounds of it, your dad has no clue where they are. Avery was smart to lead him away from here. To lure him into a trap." He smiled. "She's strong. For now, we wait."

"Like hell." He jerked free of Ryder's hold and turned to Rico. "Would you stand by if he'd taken Yolanda?" He nodded to the woman he'd seen Rico kissing earlier that day.

"Hell no," Rico barked out.

Yolanda nudged him towards the doorway. "If you get yourself killed, I'm not moving in with you."

Rico smiled. "Deal." He looked at Lucas. "Well, come on. Let's go help save your woman."

"Know where this cabin is?" he asked Rico as they darted outside into the dark.

"Nope," Rico answered.

"I do," Ryder said, catching up with them. "It's down the pathway." He motioned to the dimly lit cobblestone walkway.

They ran until they heard Avery's loud voice, then the three of them stilled.

"I told them they could stay here until their house was done being fumigated," she was saying loudly. "I'm not sure they're home just now."

The cottage was dark, and Avery was standing just outside the doorway under the lamp.

When had it gotten dark? He'd been so oblivious to everything except his work. Hell, he hadn't even seen Diego stroll into the kitchen until he'd bumped into him. He'd been about ready to complain to whoever was in his way when he'd spotted the gun.

Then, someone in the kitchen had dropped a plate and screamed. After that, everyone froze. Time seemed to stop altogether. His hearing had dulled. His eyesight had narrowed until all he could see was Diego standing in front of him, dressed in black, with his grandfather's military-style rifle strapped to his chest.

Did this mean Diego had done something to his grandfather? Was he still alive? Shit, he should have asked someone to check on the old man.

Lucas knew that there was no way in hell the older man would have allowed his son to take his guns. Never. Not if he was still alive.

"She's running out of time. She can't stall him much longer," Rico whispered.

Sure enough, he could see that Diego was losing his patience.

"I know I have the keys here somewhere," Avery said, sounding a little nervous as she flipped through the small clutch purse she'd carried that day for the wedding.

"Dad, let her go," Lucas said loudly, stepping into the light.

His father jerked around to face him. At that same moment, the door to the cabin flung open, and dark hands reached out and snagged Avery, pulling her inside in one quick motion. He saw a flash of her brother's face and knew that whatever happened now, at least she was safe.

"What in the hell have you done with them? You keep spreading these lies," Diego said. "Why? I didn't do anything to you."

"You didn't have to," he shot back. "Then again, I wasn't the one you wanted."

Diego's eyes turned harder. "She's mine. My blood. I can do what I want—"

"No! You can't! Lucas shouted. "She's not yours. Never was. You can't own someone. You can't take what you want, just because she's your daughter."

"It's not like that. We're... I'm meant to..." He shook his head, seemingly confused. "I never laid a hand on her, boy." His father sneered as if he was back under control. He was switching between confusion and control, making Lucas wonder if the man was mentally unstable. "You know it. You lied to get me locked up."

"I didn't lie," he said softly as he took a step backward. "And you will never see her or me again." Just as his father raised the rifle towards him, Lucas jumped back into the darkness and the bushes that surrounded the cottage. He landed in the soft sand just as two shots rang out. The first bullet hit the cobblestone pathway a few feet away from where he'd just stood. The second bullet hit his father directly in the chest, dropping him to his knees.

"I never touched her," his father said several times before falling face first into the pathway. Seconds later, Aiden and Tom appeared from the cottage door. Weapons were drawn and aimed at his father's body. Tom quickly unstrapped the rifle from his father while Aiden rolled him over and started administering first aid.

"Lucas!" Avery shouted from somewhere behind him.

He climbed out of the bush he'd jumped into and caught her in his arms as she came flying towards him.

"You're okay?" she cried, holding onto him.

"You're okay?" he asked, desperately wishing that it were lighter so that he could see for himself that she was unharmed.

"I'm fine." She touched his face. "I'm sorry," she said as tears rolled down her cheeks.

"You scared me." He pulled her back into his arms.

"I had to get him away from everyone," she said into his chest.

"Yeah, I know." He sighed. "I should have thought of it myself."

"Are you okay?" Wyatt said, stopping near them.

"Yeah," he answered, just as a group of people rushed towards them.

"Was that a gunshot?" someone asked.

"Are you okay?" Yolanda rushed to Rico.

His entire kitchen staff huddled around them, along with a handful of wedding guests.

"We're all fine," Avery said, getting everyone's attention. He felt her shake in his arms and knew she needed a moment to compose herself. Most likely, she didn't want anyone else's evening to be spoiled. "Now, everyone please head back inside. Let's leave Tom and Aiden to do their job." She nodded at her dad, who walked past them so he could help apply first aid to Diego.

"Later, we're going to have a serious talk about you putting yourself in danger," her father said as he passed them. Then he turned to him. "I'm glad you're okay."

"Can you have someone go check on my grandfather?" he asked, then rattled off his address. "That's his gun." He motioned to the weapon Tom held.

"Sure, we'll let you know," Tom answered. He relayed Lucas's grandfather's address into his radio.

"You don't think..." Avery started.

"I'm not sure," he said, taking her hand in his.

"Come on." Avery tugged on him. "You have a lot of

guests to serve dinner. Until we know, at least we can keep busy."

"Right." He walked back down the pathway holding her hand and felt the moment they both stopped shaking.

"Do you think he'll survive?" she asked when they reached the door.

"I don't care." He sighed. "Either way, he's never going to get out now."

"No, I don't suppose so." She smiled. "I love you."

He tilted his head, then smiled. "I love you." He kissed her.

When they stepped into the kitchen, his mother and Sophia rushed to his side. To his surprise, his grandfather stepped forward and wrapped his arms around all of them.

"Grand-pap?" he cried, holding onto the man as he felt his entire body start to shake again.

"I was having dinner with your mom, Graig, and Sophia. We came to town to see their new house." His grandfather motioned to where Graig stood, his arms wrapped around his mother.

"Go get some air and spend a few moments with your family. We've got this." Rico shoved him towards the back door.

"I'm going to head in and let everyone know I'm okay," Avery said with a smile, then she leaned up and kissed him. "I'm glad you're all safe," she said to his family.

She hugged each one of them before heading back into the party. The moment Avery disappeared through the door, his grandfather turned to him.

"You'd be a fool not to marry that woman and soon," his grandfather said loudly.

His entire kitchen staff chuckled.

"I agree," Sophia chimed in.

"Yeah, I'm working on it." He nodded. "Come on, I'll fill you all in on what happened."

They sat out on a picnic table under some string lights as he filled his family in on how Avery had sacrificed herself for everyone else.

Upon hearing this, his grandfather called him a fool for not dropping to his knees and begging her to marry him on the spot.

Tom interrupted the conversation to tell him that his grandfather's place had been broken into, and they were concerned for his well-being. They all relaxed when they found out that the old man was there.

The shot to the chest hadn't killed his father. The old man was in an ambulance on his way back to Edgeview, where he'd have surgery.

As Lucas said, he no longer cared what happened to the man. Whether he lived or died, he'd never be a part of their lives again.

"I should have sold those guns years ago," his grandfather said. "I don't want them back," he told Tom. "Do whatever you want with them. Melt them down for all I care. I only had them to protect myself against my son. I never thought he'd break in and get ahold of them. Never thought he'd try to use them on anyone." He shook his head and, for the first time in Lucas's life, he saw the old man cry.

"We're okay," Sophia said, wrapping her arms around him. "We're all safe now."

"Yes," Lucas agreed as he held onto his sister. "Thanks to Avery," he added softly.

"You'd better get back inside. Aren't you in charge tonight?" Graig said finally.

He nodded. "Why don't you all come in for some food?"

"There you are," Avery said just outside the doorway.

"Everyone's asking after you," she told him. "Come on inside. You all are welcome to join the party."

"We couldn't," his mother started.

"Oh, please? I've never been to a wedding before," Sophia begged. Avery rushed over and wrapped her arms around his sister. "I love your dress," Sophia said as she hugged Avery.

"Thanks, come on inside. They're just about to serve the main course. Which is why your brother is needed." She winked at him.

He stood up and followed his family back inside.

The moment the food was served, everyone in the room clapped for him and his staff. He'd never felt anything as amazing as having an entire roomful of people, an entire town almost, treat him with such kindness.

He'd never imagined he'd ever have anything this wonderful.

Avery sat across the room from him, next to her brother, and looked at him with such love. She had been willing to sacrifice herself for everyone here. No wonder. She loved every person in the room and there was no doubt they all loved her just as much.

Over the next two hours, many people approached him or found him in the kitchen to tell him how wonderful the food was. Everyone said they couldn't wait for the grand opening on Tuesday.

His mother, Graig, his sister, and grandfather left shortly after eating their meals with the rest of the guests. His mother still moved slowly due to her broken ribs. His sister's cast, which had been replaced with a removable one since she had broken her first one twice, was due to be removed in a few weeks.

Summer was ending. His restaurant, his dream, would finally be realized in just a few short days.

Until then, he knew that he had to make things solid with Avery. His grandfather was right. He should have gotten down on his knee the moment he'd seen that Avery was okay and proposed to her. The sooner he made her a permanent part of his life, the better.

Only, he knew that most women liked big romantic gestures. Just like hiding the name of his restaurant and waiting for the grand opening, some things took time. Preparation.

With a renewed desire and focus, he spent the rest of the evening plotting. He was interrupted by Kara, who shoved her phone in front of his face. There on the screen was a picture of a tiny baby.

"Meet your cousin once removed, James George Stevens," Kara said with a smile.

He reached over, took the phone, and laughed at the beautiful baby. Then he hugged Kara as she laughed.

Going forward, he was determined to make his and Avery's future together the very best. She deserved so much more than he could give her. Yet he was the one she loved. How had he gotten so lucky?

It took him all the next day to finally come up with a plan.

Then it took a lot of sneaking around and secret phone calls to put that plan into action. It would all be worth it to hear that one tiny word from Avery. To hear her say yes.

Chapter Twenty-Three

Avery couldn't have imagined that in one single week, she'd have so many wonderful days. Sure, there had been a few bumps. Almost getting shot or losing the man she loved was a huge bump, but they had survived, and now that they were on the other side, much stronger because of it.

There was a new baby in town, James George Stevens, born on her brother and Hannah's wedding day. What a fun and amazing surprise.

Since she and Lucas were officially living together, she'd allowed his mother and Sophia to take over the cottage until their house was ready.

Graig had wanted them all to move in together, but Emily was determined to wait until they could all move into their new house together.

She and Lucas had spent the entire Sunday after the wedding moving Emily's and Sophia's things into a storage unit since their old house had sold quickly.

Lucas didn't close on his new place for a few more

weeks, but already they were looking at furniture online together.

By Tuesday morning, everything was ready for the grand opening at eleven that morning.

Lucas had been so busy the entire day before that he'd barely said two words to her. Then again, she'd been busy too. She'd only left her office twice that entire day.

When she'd woken up that morning, Lucas was already downstairs. He'd left her a sweet note telling her that he wanted her to sleep in and wanted her to know that he loved her. When she was ready, breakfast would be ready for her downstairs.

After showering and putting on a pair of black jeans and a new blouse that she'd purchased at Classy and Sassy Boutique just for the grand opening, she headed downstairs.

Before she entered the kitchen, she glanced around the empty dining room. Soon the place would be packed with people she loved. Family and friends who would come to support Lucas. Come to try something new in town. Come because, whether he knew it or not, Lucas was one of them now.

Opening the kitchen door, she stilled when she saw Lucas standing in the middle of the kitchen, holding out a single red rose toward her.

"Good morning," he said with a smile.

She frowned. "Where is everyone?"

He chuckled. "They won't be here for a few hours." He motioned to a small table he'd set up in the middle of the kitchen. "I thought we'd enjoy one last quiet breakfast here together."

Smiling, she took the rose from him and sat down in the chair he held out for her.

"This morning, to start, we have fresas con crema," he said in a thick accent as he moved quickly and set a small dish of strawberries in cream in front of her. "Followed by huevos chilaquiles with bacon and fresh avocado." He wiggled his eyebrows.

"You never cease to amaze me." She sighed after taking her first bite of the food.

"To us." He held up a champagne glass. She picked her own up and tapped it with his.

"There is one more item on the menu," he said before she could take a sip.

"Oh?" She held the glass to her lips.

He nodded to the glass. Frowning, she looked into it and stilled. There at the bottom of the glass, sitting in bubbly champagne, sat a silver ring. The bubbles distorted it, making it look like a round blob.

Then he moved over beside her and got down on his knee. He took her hand in his.

"Avery Ann Austin, will you marry me?" he said, and suddenly she realized he was nervous. Very nervous.

Laughing, she nodded, and in one gulp she swallowed the liquid and tipped the ring out onto her palm.

Lucas grabbed her napkin and wiped the ring off as she held out her hand. When he slipped it on her finger, she smiled at the beautiful antique ring. It was her dream ring. How?

"Ruby told me that you'd wanted it back when you worked there but couldn't afford it. She saved it for you all this time," he said, still holding her hand.

"I've wanted it for years." She held it to her heart. "How did you know?"

He laughed and hugged her. "I didn't. Hannah did. She

told me that I'd be a fool to let you go. When I told her I was going to ask you, after I'd already asked your father the other night at the wedding, she told me about the ring."

"You..." She shook her head in disbelief. "They already know?"

He nodded. "Small town. Remember?"

She smiled. "I love you." She kissed him.

"I love you. Fiancée." He smiled. "That's not the only surprise I have for you. Now that we're official, I can let you in on the biggest secret I have."

She gasped. "The name?"

He nodded and walked over to the hook by the back door. She watched him remove his white chef shirt and pull it on.

Squinting, she stood up and walked over to see the name that was embroidered on his chest.

"Pride Pueblo Cocina," she read as she ran her finger over the perfect stitching in blue. "Pride Town Kitchen."

He smiled. "Do you think everyone will like it?"

She nodded, feeling her eyes water again. "I think they're going to love it." She hugged him and kissed him.

"Tonight, there are a few more surprises," he assured her. "But I'll save those for later."

"I can't imagine anything else that could make this day any more perfect."

He laughed. "I'll take that challenge. Now, let's eat. We have a full day ahead of us."

"I have a few surprises for you too," she said with a grin.

"Oh?" He moved closer to her.

"Later." She laughed and sat back down to enjoy their breakfast.

Over the next few hours, whenever an employee would

show up, Lucas would hand them a personalized embroidered shirt, letting them all in on the surprise of the restaurant's name.

Rico was finally able to unpack the newly printed menus, complete with the logo and name, and place them all in their protective sleeves.

The employees gathered around the bar an hour before opening and unveiled the mural that Elle had painted on the bar. It had the logo—a sun setting over the Pacific waters with a sombrero on it—and the name, Pride Pueblo Cocina, printed underneath.

The bright greens, oranges, and reds really made the blue bar stand out and look much happier.

"Boss, when do we unveil the sign?" Rico asked.

"When there's a crowd outside," he answered. "For now, we still have work to do."

Just then there was a knock on the door.

"Here's my first surprise," she said, rushing to open the front door for his grandfather.

She kissed the older man on his cheek and then stood back as he and his bandmates shuffled inside.

"Grand-pap what are you..." Lucas broke off. "You're going to play today?"

"We wouldn't miss it for the world," his grandfather said with a laugh.

Lucas looked at her. "This is your doing?" She nodded and he wrapped his arms around her. "Thank you."

"All it took to convince him was the other night. He says they're short a player or two, but they'll make do." She sighed as the band set up in the corner stage area outside. "I did promise them free drinks after they're done." She winced. "I hope they don't drink us out of tequila."

Lucas laughed. "I think we have plenty."

Within the next half hour, a line started forming outside. When the crowd filled the street, she knew it was time. Heading to the back, she grabbed Lucas's hand and got everyone's attention.

"In less than five minutes, we're going to open those doors," she told everyone. "We're going to head up and unveil the sign. Once we're done, Rico, you're on door duty. Every single person who walks in that door is to receive a loyalty keychain card." She held hers up and smiled. "Great idea." She winked at Lucas, who smiled at her. "Also give them the explanation of the rewards for loyal customers. Free drinks, free tacos, and more. We all know the drill. Smiles, friendly faces, and great food." Several of them repeated after her, and she laughed. Then she turned to Lucas. "Say something." She nudged him.

"Avery is so much better at this than I am." He paused. "Don't screw this up," he added and everyone laughed. "Good luck today and try to have fun. This is your familia. Enjoy." He took her hand and started heading up to the roof.

"Ready?" he said, stopping just inside the door to the rooftop.

"Ready," she agreed after taking a deep breath.

"There's one more surprise I have for you behind this door. One that I hope we can enjoy for many nights to come." He lifted her ringed finger to his lips and brushed a kiss over her knuckles.

She frowned and then gasped when he flung open the door.

"How?" She walked out on the rooftop. Instead of the old tar roof, there was a perfectly level deck flooring. Wood posts stood along the sides, holding lights strung over the entire deck. There were even potted planters filled with colorful flowers and several picnic tables and lounge chairs with cushions that sat around gas firepits. The space made the little patio downstairs look small. "How did you do this so quickly?"

"Well, it wasn't quick. Parker and his crew could only work when you were busy with your brother's wedding or stuck in your office all day. They've been working on this since the first time I brought you up here and I saw how much it meant to you." He smiled. "Surprised?"

"It's amazing," she said, and then the sounds of the crowd below them hit her. "We'd better hurry." She glanced around one more time. "We could host parties up here."

"I know," he said with a laugh. "Parker has assured me it can hold at least a hundred and fifty people."

"I love it." She hugged and kissed him. "And I think we're going to need to use it tonight."

"Yeah, I think so," he said when they reached the front of the building.

"Welcome," she said, trying to get everyone's attention.

Lucas handed her a microphone and motioned for her to try again.

She had to lean a little over the high wall, but when she spoke into the microphone, everyone stood back and looked up at her.

"Lucas and I"—she glanced at him and he nodded—"first off, we just got engaged!" She held up their joined hands as everyone below them cheered. "Secondly, we want to thank everyone for coming out today. We have some amazing surprises in store for you, but first..." She handed the microphone to Lucas, who leaned over the wall to be seen.

"Hola. I want to be the first to welcome you to Pride

Pueblo Cocina," he said as he and Avery tugged on the string that held a thick black sheet over the sign. Lucas had removed the plastic late the night before.

The sheet moved away and everyone standing in the streets cheered as the front doors flew open.

Also by Jill Sanders

The Pride Series

Finding Pride

Discovering Pride

Returning Pride

Lasting Pride

Serving Pride

Red Hot Christmas

My Sweet Valentine

Return To Me

Rescue Me

A Pride Christmas

The Secret Series

Secret Seduction

Secret Pleasure

Secret Guardian

Secret Passions

Secret Identity

Secret Sauce

Secret Obsession

Secret Desire

Secret Charm

Secret Santa

The West Series

Loving Lauren

Taming Alex

Holding Haley

Missy's Moment

Breaking Travis

Roping Ryan

Wild Bride

Corey's Catch

Tessa's Turn

Saving Trace

Christmas Holly

Maggie's Match

The Grayton Series

Last Resort

Someday Beach

Rip Current

In Too Deep

Swept Away

High Tide

Sunset Dreams

Lucky Series

Unlucky In Love

Sweet Resolve

Best of Luck

A Little Luck

Christmas Wish

Silver Cove Series

Silver Lining

French Kiss

Happy Accident

Hidden Charm

A Silver Cove Christmas

Sweet Surrender

Second Chances

Dancing on Air

Entangled Series – Paranormal Romance

The Awakening

The Beckoning

The Ascension

The Presence

The Calling

The Chosen

The Beyond

The Void

Haven, Montana Series

Closer to You

Never Let Go

Holding On

Coming Home

The Hard Way

Never Again

Pride Oregon Series

A Dash of Love

My Kind of Love

Season of Love

Tis the Season

Dare to Love

Where I Belong

Because of Love

A Thing Called Love

First Comes Love

Someone to Love

Fools in Love

FindingLove

Christmas Joy

Always My Love

Forever My Love

Searching for Love

Wildflowers Series

Summer Nights

Summer Heat

Summer Secrets

Summer Fling

Summer's End

Summer Wish

Summer Breeze

Summer Ride

Distracted Series

Wake Me

Tame Me

Save Me

Dare Me

Stand Alone Books

Twisted Rock

Hope Harbor

Raven Falls

Angel Bluff

Day Break

Diamonds in the Mud

For a complete list of books:

http://JillSanders.com

About the Author

Jill Sanders is a New York Times, USA Today, and international bestselling author of Sweet Contemporary Romance, Romantic Suspense, Western Romance, and Paranormal Romance novels. With over 90 books in eleven series, translations into several different languages, and audiobooks there's plenty to choose from. Look for Jill's bestselling stories wherever romance books are sold or visit her at jillsanders.com

Jill comes from a large family with six siblings, including an identical twin. She was raised in the Pacific Northwest and later relocated to Colorado for college and a successful IT career before discovering her talent for writing sweet and sexy page-turners. After Colorado, she decided to move south, living in Texas and now making her home along the Emerald Coast of Florida. You will find that the settings of several of her series are inspired by her time spent living in these areas. She has two sons and off-set the testosterone in her house by adopting three furry little ladies that provide her company while she's locked in her writing cave. She enjoys heading to the beach, hiking, swimming, wine-tasting, and pickleball with her husband, and of course writing. If you have read any of her books, you may also notice that there is a love of food, especially sweets! She has been blamed for a few added pounds by her assistant, editor, and fans... donuts or pie anyone?

facebook.com/JillSandersBooks

x.com/JillMSanders

amazon.com/Jill-Sanders/e/B009M2NFD6?tag=jillm-com-20

bookbub.com/authors/jill-sanders

instagram.com/jillsandersauthor

tiktok.com/@jillsandersauthor